BROKEN CURSE

THE MARKED WOLF TRILOGY

JEN L. GREY

CHAPTER ONE

Emma

My heart pounded in my ears as I took deep breaths to calm myself down. When my cousin walked into this house for breakfast, I would call his ass out on what he was doing behind everyone's backs.

Babe, what's wrong? Aidan stepped into the den where I'd been pacing since everyone had finally gotten up. Concern filled his golden eyes, and his short dark hair was messy from sleep. He had slipped on some jeans, which hugged his ass and thighs, and his dark red shirt molded to his muscles. He was several inches taller than me and large.

If I hadn't been so upset, I would have very likely been drooling. *I'll tell you everything soon.* I wasn't sure I could get it out and maintain control. Anger had been my primary fuel for the past couple of hours.

Remus was deflating his and Ivory's blow-up mattress, and the air was blowing his brown hair a little as it left. His muscles contracted through his shirt as he put the mattress in its bag. His green eyes scanned his mate up and down.

Normally, it would have made me smile to see them so happy, but not today. Finn had ruined that for me.

Beatrice entered the room with her brown dress flowing behind her, making her appear younger than her mid-forties. Her hair was the same shade as her daughter's, but her eyes were a paler purple. "Wow, you guys sure know how to pick up after yourselves. I wish you'd been around to teach Amethyst a few things."

Amethyst strolled into the room, her violet eyes bright and a smile on her face. "Oh, stop it, Mom." Her smile fell, and her eyes locked right on me. "What's wrong?"

That was the question of the hour.

Aidan frowned at me. "I just asked her the same thing."

The front door opened, and Sage, Samuel, and Finn walked into the room. That was all it took for me to unload.

"Hey, *cousin*," I emphasized the word with so damn much hate.

Finn's amber eyes widened. "Hey?" He tilted his head as he scanned the room for clues about what was going on. His auburn hair was messier than usual, probably from not sleeping well after betraying us. He was almost as tall as Aidan, but not as muscular. He was all witch, which didn't do him any favors. His shirt was baggier than the shirts of the wolf shifters, but I watched him as if he were prey. Because of that, I saw his shoulders stiffen.

"Are you okay?" Samuel pulled his shoulder-length chestnut hair into a man bun, his forehead creased with worry. His sage eyes were wise beyond his years even though he didn't act wisely most of the time. I'd met him a few weeks after school had started at a tailgate party. He was a junior, but that felt like a lifetime ago.

"No. No, I'm not."

"That's pretty clear." Sage approached me and

frowned. Her eyes were the same color as Samuel's, but her hair was dark brown. She was the shortest among us, but she had unquestionable strength. "What happened?"

"Mom, I'm sure ..." Samuel trailed off when Sage gave him the "mom" eye.

"It was strange." I glanced into the den and met the eyes of the four girls who were here because of me. They trusted me, and they deserved to know, just like the priestess and the coven. "I couldn't sleep last night, so I went for a walk and overheard a very interesting conversation."

Finn stepped back, bumping into Samuel. Finn turned to run around him, but the angry shifter closest to him grabbed his arm.

"Logan, make sure he stays here." If I'd been more rational, I wouldn't have commanded that. Logan and Gabby had been raised in a pack that had only tolerated them. They had anger and trust issues, which Logan had proved when he'd killed Honor's pack alpha while we'd been helping her and Ada escape. Our goal had been to find each marked girl without causing too big of a scene, so killing a fucking alpha was a huge-ass deal.

"With pleasure." The freaky shifter grinned, and the scar from his nose to his right ear looked even more sinister. His hair was white, but not from age since he was right around twenty. His blue eyes were so light that the iris was sometimes difficult to distinguish from the sclera.

"What did you do, boy?" Beatrice's voice and hands shook.

Finn shook his head. "Nothing ..."

"Oh, wow. That was a big lie." Gabby waved her hand in front of her nose and squinted her bright blue eyes, which always seemed to glow. She then flipped her black hair over her shoulder. "It's rotten in here."

"Shifters can smell a lie," Ivory said, frowning. Her pale hand took Remus's. Her brown hair was so long it spilled between them like a curtain.

"What did you do?" Beatrice asked again, emphasizing each word.

"Let me fill you in since he obviously won't." Unadulterated rage consumed me. "He was on the phone with Prescott."

"Whoa." Aidan's jaw clenched. "The Hallowed Guild member who's roommates with your ex-boyfriend?"

It sounded like forever ago when he put it like that. I'd dated Jacob for over two years, but he'd never held a candle to Aidan. I hadn't understood, at fourteen when we would sneak to the border and risk the wrath of our packs, why we'd thrown caution to the wind. It had taken seeing him again at eighteen to figure it all out. "Yes. Your father's ally pack is looking to take the marked wolves down."

Sage turned toward the boy she considered a son, even if it wasn't biologically. "Why were you talking to them?"

"Because he's going to act as their informant as long as the pack promises to let him kill Aidan's father and doesn't attack me or the coven." How he could be so selfish and stupid was beyond me. "And he actually believes them."

"So, what? You were going to allow them to kill my mate?" Logan tightened his hands on Finn as his protective mate senses took over.

Finn winced. "It's nothing personal."

"Are you that big of a moron?" Aidan clenched his hand into a fist. "Do you really think they'll keep their word? You hate on wolf shifters all the time, but you're going to trust one of the most corrupt ones?"

"You're only saying that to save your father," Finn said through clenched teeth.

"Honestly, I'm not sure about that." Aidan rubbed his forehead. "But Prescott wants you to kill him so he won't have to. It'll make it easier for him to ascend to the top of the Hallowed Guild ranks if you kill my father and Prescott kills the girls."

"Out of everyone, you should be the most thankful." Finn lifted his chin and stared down his nose at my mate. "Don't you want to protect her?"

"But I'm not protected. They're still going to try to kill me." It was like he couldn't see reason. "You can't trust them."

"That's funny coming from you." Finn's nose wrinkled in disgust. "Your fucking mate is part of the society that wants you all dead."

"Well, hell, so are we." Remus pointed to himself and Ivory. "But that mark changed everything." He gestured to Ivory's ear. "No mate can kill their beloved."

"Aw, that's actually kind of sweet." Ada's dark eyes met those of her best friend, Honor. "Maybe not all men are pigs, but this one definitely is." She motioned back at Finn.

Ada and Honor were clearly from the same pack. They both had dark olive skin, dark eyes, and brown hair. The only difference was that Honor's hair was darker, and she was slightly taller than her friend. The similar looks probably had everything to do with their pack keeping to their own kind and not intermingling with humans.

"Maybe someone else here is conspiring and it's not me?" Finn glanced back at me. "Have you ever considered that?"

"Finn, just stop." I was done with people angrily pointing fingers at everyone but themselves over their shortcomings. "This won't bring your parents back. This hate ... this anger ... you have to let it go, or you'll wind up making stupid mistakes. You'll get other people hurt, and then what? You think you'll be okay with it, but you're in a dangerous cycle, and you need to stop."

"You don't know anything about me," Finn sneered at me.

"No, she's right." Beatrice walked over and took my side, both literally and physically. "We've been worried about you letting all this negative energy saturate you, but you'd been through so much. We didn't want to make things worse. But we were wrong. We've let you go too far."

"What does that mean?" he asked with fear. "Are you banishing me?"

"That's our point." Sage sighed. "Of course we aren't banishing you. Can't you see? We all love you, but there will be repercussions this time."

So that's what he's afraid of? It had taken this confrontation for me to realize what plagued him. *He's afraid no one loves him, and he's trying to prove he's worthy.*

Yeah, it's similar to how Logan and Gabby are acting. Aidan's voice was still full of anger. *But if his decisions hurt you, I will kill that asshole.*

Though I couldn't blame him for wanting to protect me at any cost, I wouldn't let him kill for me. Whether Finn realized it, he was the only family I had left too, and I didn't plan on losing him. I just had to knock some sense into him.

Finn glanced at Beatrice, waiting for his leader to speak. "So, what will it be?"

"Actually, Emma is our future leader, so it's up to her." Beatrice faced me, her eyes turning a darker shade of purple. "Tell him your decision."

Okay, I hadn't expected that, but she was right. I had to start acting like a leader, not just to the four marked girls but to both witches and wolves. This was my legacy. "You aren't allowed to know what we're up to."

"What?" Finn frowned. "Look, I promise I won't tell them anything."

"We can't risk it." Besides, I didn't believe him. Yes, he didn't smell of the sulfur that indicated a lie, but that only meant his intentions were pure at this moment. Who knew how he'd feel later on today or, hell, even next week? "Until you can prove you've changed, you cannot be part of the prophecy, and you will no longer be kept in the loop."

"But that's not ..."

I didn't care to hear his response. "Logan, let him go." I laced some alpha will into my voice, making it clear I expected him to obey me.

Aidan tensed beside me, ready to come to my aid.

It surprised us both when Logan listened.

"You better be glad that's all you're missing out on." Logan dropped his hand and glared at Finn. "If anything happens to my mate, I'll consider you responsible, and I will get even."

Finn swallowed hard, and I almost laughed. He was finally afraid. Good.

"Well, as fun as this is, I think it's time we get to the witch's diary." My eyes went back to Finn. "I guess we'll see you later today."

"But I didn't have any breakfast," Finn pouted.

"Then, you'd better go back to your house and figure out how to make some." Beatrice straightened her shoulders and nodded in my direction. "She's spoken."

Finn's mouth dropped open, and when he tried to catch Sage's or Samuel's eyes, they diverted their gazes to the ground.

"Fine." Finn stomped out the door and slammed it shut in his wake.

I hated doing that to Finn, but my hands were tied, and right now, there were more important things to focus on. "Now, let's get some breakfast and see what this diary has to say next."

An uneasy feeling settled in my stomach as if we were still missing a piece to the puzzle. The feeling had to be connected to what had gone down with Finn. What else could it be?

CHAPTER TWO

After Finn had left with grand theatrics, the room fell silent. I wished things could be different, but he was too much of a liability.

You did the right thing. Aidan took my hand and squeezed it comfortingly. *He has to earn our trust again.*

Maybe we should've let him earn it in the first place. There had been so many red flags, and I'd naïvely ignored them all. He was so angry, but hell, he'd fought against Prescott's pack. So how had their little treaty even begun?

"Well, that was enlightening." Samuel blew out a breath and shrugged off the thin maroon jacket he'd been wearing since the mornings were getting cooler as winter approached.

"Samuel," his mother chastised. "Don't even try to be funny right now."

"That's how he copes." Aidan shrugged. "Better that than crying."

The witch did have a soft spot that made him even more endearing.

"So, you're telling me that one of you has been in

cahoots with the wolves that want to kill us?" Gabby barked out a humorless laugh. "Maybe we were better off on our own."

"Gabby, stand down." I'd probably come off sterner than I'd meant to, but I didn't want to deal with any more drama this morning. Finn had been enough.

"On your own, you wouldn't have survived," Ivory's soft voice was strong. "Believe me, we were part of the society. They will mobilize everything they can to track us down. At least, together, we can potentially fulfill the curse—er, prophecy and bring them to their knees."

"And I was part of the original alpha's pack and grew up as an important member of The Hallowed Guild." Aidan glared at Gabby, his golden eyes glowing. "So that's how I know you'd have no chance at surviving alone. We have to figure out the next steps so we can take the society down."

The front door opened, and Beth, Coral, and Rowan entered the house.

Beth's blue eyes landed on mine, and immediately, she knew something was wrong. She crossed the room toward me, her royal blue hair bouncing with each step. Her black shirt bunched around her shoulders, revealing her anxiety. "What happened?"

Beatrice pinched the bridge of her nose. "Apparently, we have a traitor on our hands."

"Wait ..." Coral took inventory of everyone in the room. "Finn's gone, so ..."

"Yes, it was him." Amethyst frowned and ran her fingers through her long blonde hair.

Logan lifted a hand in the air. "Aren't you an empath?"

I didn't like what he was insinuating. "What the hell are you getting at?"

"That she should've known," Gabby said as she stood next to her mate, arms crossed over her chest.

"She helped save us." Honor leaned back against the wall, her dark hair contrasting against the warm-colored wallpaper.

Logan rocked on his heels. "Maybe it's a ruse."

Beatrice's eyes narrowed. "My daughter—"

"Stop," Amethyst interrupted. "It's a good question."

"You have nothing to prove." I hated that she felt like she had to explain herself. She was one of the most sincere people I'd ever known. "You were a part of saving them just like we were."

"No, it's good to question things." Amethyst paced the room as she collected herself. "Ever since Finn was a child, he's been in constant turmoil. Hurt, anger, confusion—those have been his key feelings all the time, and I didn't get a different read off him."

"He's been like this since he was a child?" Sunny sank onto the couch. "That's horrible."

Gabby placed a hand on her hip. "Well, it doesn't excuse his betrayal."

"I find it interesting that someone like you would say that." Ever since we'd picked them up, Gabby and Logan had reminded me of Finn. They had so much anger in them as well.

"What are you getting at?" Logan asked and took one step toward me, but Aidan tensed, ready to attack.

"I think it's pretty obvious. You and Gabby have a lot in common with him." Coral's long red hair cascaded down her shoulders as her crystal blue eyes met Logan's gaze head-on. "So before passing judgment, maybe look in a mirror."

A proud smile crossed Rowan's face. The only difference between her and Coral was that Rowan's red hair was more orange, and she had twenty years on her daughter.

Aidan arched an eyebrow, flicking his focus between the two shifters. "If you don't like how Finn acts, you need to take a long hard look at yourselves. You may find some common characteristics with him."

They both tensed.

"He's right, but let's not fight." They needed a wake-up call, and maybe they were finally getting it. We should probably have continued down that path, but my patience was up. "Everyone is here, so let's open up that diary and see what we need to do."

"Sounds good. Let me go grab the book." Beatrice headed down the hallway to her room.

I didn't blame her for not keeping the diary out in the open. Even though I trusted these seven new shifters, the witches needed to guard their books, which were meant to stay within the coven.

"So, what are we supposed to do?" Sunny asked as she rubbed her hands along her jeans.

"The pages near the back are blank." She hadn't been part of the locator spell with the maps, so I couldn't reference that. "The wording suggests that all five marked girls need to bleed on the first blank page. It will then reveal the next steps to fulfilling the prophecy."

She nodded. "Oh, wow."

"So... similar to the locator spell?" Remus asked and wrapped his arm around his mate's waist.

"Yes." It was supposed to be that simple.

"All magic requires a sacrifice." Amethyst lifted her hand and glanced at her finger. "Blood is the universal one that works well for most, if not every spell."

"That is very true, my child." Beatrice carried out the

old leather-bound diary. The binding was worn, revealing its age. "And here it is." She sat on the couch, laying the book on the coffee table. "Please surround me."

The five of us followed her instructions. I sat on one side of Beatrice with Ivory on the other. The other three sat on the ground around the pages.

Aidan stood behind where I sat on the couch, placing a hand on my shoulder.

It meant everything in the world to have him by my side, especially after all the shit we had to go through to get here. He'd turned his back on his family to be my mate and be here for me.

"Here we are." Beatrice pointed to the blank pages. Her hands shook as she held them down. "It is such an amazing honor to be alive and part of this history."

When they made comments like that, it reminded me how important this whole thing was. It was the complete opposite in The Hallowed Guild. They despised us, and killing us was a means to an end.

I stared at the blank pages, nervous that something bad would happen. I didn't know much about magic yet. Yes, mine had been uncovered by freeing the black void inside me, but it hadn't been unleashed. If Aidan and me bonding had caused that country-wide earthquake, there was no telling what this would do, but there was no turning back.

They're looking for you to guide them. Aidan gently patted my shoulder, bringing me back to the present.

He hadn't been kidding. All four of the marked women were looking directly at me. "Let's go in the order we found everyone in." Which meant I was up first. It only seemed right since I was asking them to spill their blood too.

I took a deep breath and bit into my finger. I held it over

the blank page and turned it over, allowing several drops to fall on the page. Then in order, the girls did the same thing.

The witches crowded in, wanting to see what would happen.

Our blood converged and began swirling. It circled over and over again, reminding me of a loading screen on a laptop. We all watched it intently, ready for the great reveal. The circle pulsed and shot off like a firework on the page.

I was ready for the words to reveal themselves, but instead, the blood soaked into the page and disappeared.

We all watched for a few more moments, waiting for something, anything, but nothing happened.

"What the hell?" Samuel whispered as if afraid to break the spell.

Beatrice inhaled sharply. "I ... I don't understand."

Great, was this some kind of joke? Right when I'd been about to stand and stretch my legs, dizziness hit me. The room spun so fast that my stomach churned. *Aidan, what's going on?*

What are you talking about? Concern laced each word.

The room, it's spinning. I closed my eyes, but it didn't help. I fell back against the couch, thankful I hadn't stood.

"Emma," Sunny gasped from the floor next to me.

Babe, the room isn't ... His words trailed off as darkness engulfed me.

THE SURROUNDING AIR WAS COOL, and a deep chill settled in my bones. I tried opening my eyes, but they were so damn heavy. *Aidan?*

There was no response, and the silence was deafening.

I moved my hand, but it touched nothing. I couldn't feel

anything underneath or around me. It was as if I were floating.

Was I dead? That was the only thing that made any sense.

Despite the adrenaline pulsing through me, I struggled to pry my eyes open. It took God knew how long, but eventually, the lids pulled apart.

However, it didn't change a damn thing. Solid darkness surrounded me as if my eyes were still shut.

There wasn't a breeze, yet the air around me moved. It wasn't stagnant or stale. If that wasn't creepy enough, it was filled with pure silence and scentless. I felt no sense of time.

I slowly sat and blinked hard several times, trying to make sense of what was going on. *Aidan?* I pleaded.

Silence was my only response.

There was no way in hell I would just give up and sit here and rot. I slowly stood and took a few small steps to get my bearings. Not even my tennis shoes made a noise.

"Hello?" I called out like an idiot, but I didn't have anything to lose. "Is anyone there?"

Not even an echo responded to me.

Fear crawled up my spine, and I rubbed my hands along my arms. None of this made sense.

I tried to remember the seconds before I got here, but I was drawing a blank. It was as if my past, present, and future had collided, but there was nothing to prove that.

Needing to make noise, I stomped my feet, but it didn't produce a single sound.

"Is anyone here?" At this point, I'd be ecstatic to see Jacob.

Aidan ... The Hallowed Guild ... the diary. Our blood hadn't revealed the blank pages. It all began coming back to me, almost at a snail's pace.

"I don't understand." I grabbed my hair. "We had all five of us. Are you four down here too?" Were we all trapped together? "Gabby? Ivory? Honor? Sunny?" I listed them off, hoping one of them would answer. Well, maybe I shouldn't be hoping for that.

Silence was yet again my response. Hell, I wondered if I was actually talking. "Is anyone here?"

Thunder vibrated around me—through my body, through the air, through my blood. A huge white flash zig-zagged through the room, barely missing me.

At least, I got a response this time.

A guttural cry filled the air, "You are not worthy."

Okay, maybe I'd preferred the silence. My heart hammered, and I spun around, looking for a sign of someone ... anyone. But blackness engulfed me once again.

CHAPTER THREE

Aidan

"Emma!" I rushed around the couch and cupped her gorgeous face. Her fingers were tangled in her blonde hair, and her eyes were closed. I desperately wished I could see her beautiful gray eyes again. Her lips trembled, making her cleft chin more pronounced.

Beth flew across the room and stopped right next to me. "What's wrong with her?"

"I ..." *Emma?* I kept trying to connect with her and coming up blank. "I don't know."

"Did you do something?" Gabby's accusatory tone rang clear in the room.

I looked over my shoulder for a second. "Gabby, stand down."

"But she didn't get like that until after ..." Gabby trailed off. "What if we're next?"

I didn't have time to deal with this. "Just calm your ass down. You're only making the situation worse."

Beth sighed with relief. "She's still breathing, and I can feel her pulse."

Coral walked over and placed her hands on the headrest next to Emma's head. "Can you connect with her?"

"No, it's like there's a block, but our connection is on track. It's weird." It got crazier second by second. "I can feel her, just not connect with her."

"What does that mean?" Sunny sounded breathless. "How can we help her?"

"Somebody has to know something." I met Beatrice's light purple eyes. "Can't you do something?"

"I can try." She bit her bottom lip and placed a hand on Emma's arm. She jerked her hand back as if she'd been stung. "Ouch. There's so much power coming off her."

"Then how can I touch her?" I gestured to Beth. "She touched her too."

"It's because you two aren't witches." Beatrice's eyes widened as she glanced at her daughter. "Can you feel anything coming from her?"

"She's scared. That's all I have." Amethyst rubbed her hands together. "But there isn't anything we can do ... I don't think."

———

Emma

"WHAT DO YOU WANT?" I yelled ... or at least, I thought I did.

Nothing responded.

I inhaled sharply, and the cold air hurt my lungs. Maybe this was purgatory. According to some, purgatory was worse than Hell since it was neither good nor bad. I'd never believed it until now. I could go insane here if given the chance.

There had to be a way out. I pushed my legs into a run and waited to find something.

But total blackness surrounded me.

Maybe shifting would help. I'd never felt blind before, and it unsettled me. Turning into my wolf could be the key.

I called my wolf forward, but nothing happened. She was there but inaccessible. That was when the gravity of the situation hit me directly in the gut.

My wolf couldn't help me. Was that why I could only see blackness? Was this what it was like to be fully human? I couldn't bear the thought of not having my wolf or Aidan.

"Why am I here?" I yelled at the top of my lungs and fell to my hands and knees.

It was so disconcerting because I'd stopped, but I didn't feel anything.

Fear wanted to take over, but I held on to some sense of sanity. If I lost myself, I wasn't sure what would happen. Would the person who'd spoken strike me with lightning?

"There has to be a reason I'm here." I tried to ignore the pain that came with each intake of air.

"You must ask the right question," the deep voice rang all around me again.

Oh, wow. The right question. "What am I supposed to do?"

No response yet again.

Okay, I had to think. Us combining our blood in the diary had been the last thing to happen before I'd woken up here. Did it have something to do with that? "Is this where I learn the rest of the prophecy?" Was this the next step in the puzzle?

Mocking laughter surrounded me.

Well, that wasn't a promising sign. I forced myself to my feet again, refusing to cower in front of whomever this was. They were getting a high from my weakness. "Okay, so if this isn't to reveal the next step, it has to be something else."

If I wanted out of here, I had to figure out what the right question was. Something deep inside me had known that all along, but I'd needed to get my meltdown out of the way.

I had to get some of the nervousness out of my system, so I began pacing. Maybe exercise would clear my mind. The first words the entity had spoken repeated inside my head. "You said I'm not worthy." That had to be a hint. "How do I become worthy?"

Light flashed all around me, and I shut my eyes. It had been so dark. So, this had to be what it felt like for a human when lights suddenly turned on in a room. I blinked and glanced around, taking in the entire scene.

The trees reminded me of my pack home back in Mount Juliet, Tennessee, but instead of the houses I knew, there were small log cabins similar to what we'd found in Ojai, California. "What the …"

"Watch your language, my child." The voice that had been mocking me came from right behind me. I spun around, and the breath was almost knocked out of me.

The woman was older than me, but her features were so damn similar to mine. Her hair was a light blonde; however, her eyes had more blue in them. Even though her chin was smooth and I had several inches on her, we could easily be family members.

"Who are you?" I forced my eyes to leave hers and glanced around the area.

"You should know the answer to that." The woman smiled, but it didn't meet her eyes.

"Where are we?" If I hadn't known any better, I would

have thought this was the Rogers pack lands from many hundred years ago.

"It's our home," she said slowly, and the weight of the knowledge hit me right in the chest.

"Then you're the ..." No, it couldn't be. I had to be going crazy. "... original witch." There, I'd said it.

"Very good." She nodded and took a step toward me while her long dress billowed behind her. "My name is Endora."

Knowing the original witch's name unnerved me. With the lilies in her hair and sun-kissed skin, unlike most of the pale witches now, she looked as one with nature.

"How is this possible?" Had I gone back in time, or was this a dream? Well, maybe calling it a dream was a stretch. I was talking to a dead woman after all.

"Magic never dies." The original witch spread out her arms and spun around and around. "When a witch dies, they don't go into oblivion like other races do."

"Into oblivion?" That sounded so isolating. "What about Heaven and Hell?"

"Oh, those antiquated notions." She shrugged. "I never spent much time on them since I knew I'd live forever just like you will."

"You died giving birth." This had to be a nightmare.

"In one sense, but I'm now part of nature and, in some ways, more alive than ever." She dropped her hands, walked over to a tree, and touched its bark.

I was going to drop that whole heaven-and-hell conversation because we needed to focus on the immediate issues at hand. "If I'm not worthy, how come I'm here?"

"Because you still can prove your worth. It's not hopeless ... yet." She turned back around with a huge smile on her face. "You see, I always knew you would make it closer than the others and would be the only one who would ever be able to become my retribution, so I'm here to give you a hint."

"Look, I'm not here to punish anyone. I just want wolves and witches to live in peace." It was that simple. I didn't want Aidan and me to be on the run for the rest of our lives.

"Maybe that's your goal, but by accomplishing that, you'll be solidifying my master plan." Her laugh was full of angst and hunger.

"How do we look so much alike?" I shouldn't have been worried about that, but our likeness was too uncanny not to ask.

"Because you're my great, great ..." She trailed off. "Let's just say I am your ancestor. I'm not sure how many greats should be in front of my title. It was so long ago."

"How is that possible?" I was half-witch and half-wolf.

"Well, both your mother and father are my descendants —granted, very distant family members—but they originated from me just the same." She placed a surprisingly warm hand on my arm.

"But my dad was a shifter."

"He was the product of fated mates from the Rogers and Murphy packs several years after I perished." She frowned with sadness, which turned her eyes a darker blue, eliminating any hint of gray. "The man was from the Rogers pack and my grandson. A gift from my eldest child."

"Wait ... you had another child?" No one had mentioned that before.

"It's not common knowledge. Not even that bastard Murphy alpha knew about him." She turned and stared off toward the border that separated the two packs. "A mother always protects her child."

"So, when the alpha killed your shared child, he killed the wrong one that would set the prophecy into motion." A cold realization filled me.

"See, this proves you'll be able to figure everything out." She bent down and ran her fingers along the grass.

"What kind of monster are you?" Maybe the alpha hadn't been the sicko. "You had your daughter, knowing she would die." She had the gift of foresight, so had this been her plan all along?

"No, I did not." She stiffened and stood, turning toward me with a scowl. "I would've never willingly had my child killed like that ... as if she were nothing."

"But you could see the future." It was that simple. There was no getting out of it.

She clenched her hands into fists. "The gift of foresight does not let a person see their own future or their children's. If you could see your own death, you would try to change destiny, which is not allowed. So that's why there is that one exception."

That made sense, but I'd verify it once I got back to Aidan. "Then, who fathered your other child?"

"My husband was also a witch, and he died shortly after our son's birth. That's why I found the Rogers pack for protection. The humans had found out about us and were going on a killing spree." She clutched her chest. "Little did I know that by going there for protection, I'd cause not only my death but my daughter's."

I didn't say anything, wanting her to continue.

"I wanted protection, so I looked for a strong alpha, and Murphy fit that exact mold."

"Murphy? He went by his last name?"

"No, child. The pack was named after him." She shook her head. "It was given out of respect. The next alpha took it, not only as the pack's name but as their own last name," she spat.

That blew my mind. "They worship him."

"No, they feared his version of the future." She chuckled. "He'd come to me nightly, desperate for my body."

"Okay, you can stop there." She was family, and the last thing I wanted to hear was their sordid sex details.

"Fair enough." She smirked. "Murphy would come once my son was asleep, so he never knew about him. He never cared to spend time with me during the day, but the night I told him about our baby, he told me to get rid of it. When I refused, he beat me and kicked me in my stomach to make me lose her."

My stomach revolted. Who could do that to his own child?

She held up a hand. "I don't want to get into the specifics. You've read my diary and know everything that happened from that point on." She took in a shaky breath. "So, my son was cared for by the Rogers pack just as you were. He fell in love with a female shifter, and they promised themselves to each other. That's when my plan was set into motion. You see, after what happened, I made sure another witch wouldn't go through what I had unless it was one I'd granted the prophecy to. So, I allowed my son to have one child with his wife, and I made sure it was more wolf than witch so no one would ever know outside the pack."

"But the Murphy and Rogers packs were enemies then. So how was my father a descendant?" I was still missing an important piece.

"They weren't enemies yet." She frowned. "But when my grandson fell in love with a Murphy pack shifter, tension escalated over who would be the couple's future leaders. After all, they would want to be pack members, which meant they'd have the same alpha. That was the final straw and when my grandson decided to leave the Rogers pack."

That would be yet another blow the Murphy pack had inflicted on the Rogers pack.

"You are my direct descendant. That's how you're different from the rest. You have more of my blood in you than anyone since my grandson."

"And that's why I'm the one who could be the most worthy?" That added even more pressure on me. "And why I've had the mark since birth."

"Exactly. I'd hoped the women before you would be worthy, but they weren't strong enough, despite my help." An adoring smile filled her face. "So of course, you'd be the one to get us this far. When you figure out the missing piece, you'll be unstoppable. My blood is strong."

The surrounding light dimmed, and the original witch gave me a sad smile. "Your time here is up. If you stay much longer, you won't be able to return to your body."

"Are you going to give me a hint?" She couldn't have only brought me here for a history lesson.

"There is a piece of the puzzle you're missing." She arched an eyebrow. "It can be found on each one of the girls."

"Wow, that's super helpful." My mind reeled. What the hell was I missing?

"I have faith in you." She walked into the woods as the darkness took over. "Oh, and when you figure it out, don't trust right away. My blood had to be tested, and each drop has its own demons."

"What does that mean?"

But darkness was my answer, and I began falling.

CHAPTER FOUR

Aidan

It had been the longest twenty-four hours of my life. I held Emma tightly in my arms, right against my chest, listening to her breathing and heartbeat. No one knew what was going on, but one thing was clear: whenever a witch touched her, they were shocked. They couldn't bring her back from wherever she'd gone.

My eyes were heavy, but I wouldn't dare close them. I had to make sure she was okay.

A light knock sounded on the bedroom door.

Beatrice's unique flowery smell wafted under the door. "Come in."

The door opened slowly, and she entered the room. Her eyes went straight to my mate. "Any changes?"

"No. Her breathing becomes labored from time to time, but then it evens out." I felt so damn helpless. The woman who owned my heart was in danger, and I couldn't do anything to protect her. This had always been my fear ar one of the reasons I'd left her for four years. Now, I was living my nightmare, and it wasn't even my father's fault.

"Amethyst," Beatrice called over her shoulder. "Can you come in here and tell us what you sense?"

"Sure," Amethyst replied, and soon her footsteps headed in our direction.

"I know I'll regret this..." Beatrice came over and closed her eyes. Wincing, she touched my mate. "Agh." She jerked back.

"Why does that keep happening?" Something had to be doing this to her, but who. "Is it another witch?" That was the only thing that made sense.

Amethyst's brows furrowed as she joined us in the room. "Is everything okay?"

"Is that a real question?" Of course, nothing was okay.

"Aidan, I'm sorry." Her shoulders sagged, and her kind, violet eyes darkened with guilt. "I didn't mean it like that."

I should have told her it was fine, but I couldn't. Everything was so fucked up.

"Can you read her?" Beatrice turned toward her daughter and waved her hand as if it still burned.

"She's ... confused." Amethyst's forehead lined as she stared hard at Emma. "It's strange. She's trying to figure something out."

"Do we have any clue who is doing this to her?" I needed answers.

Beatrice walked around the bed to the window that overlooked the trees. "It's going to sound crazy, but I think I do."

"Then, who is it?" Amethyst stepped toward her mother before stopping. "I have no clue who could do something so powerful."

"And that's why I said you'll think I'm crazy." Beatrice turned to face us. "But it came to me last night."

I wanted to bite out the words "Just say it," but I clenched my teeth. Rudeness probably wouldn't go over really well.

"I think it's the original witch," Beatrice said slowly as if we might be too stupid to comprehend.

"You've got to be kidding." Amethyst laughed but stopped short. "Oh ... you're not."

"Think about it. The zap we feel is foreign yet familiar, and Emma had just dropped her blood on the diary." Beatrice placed her hand on her neck. "And no one is strong like that."

"Maybe, but that sounds far-fetched." Amethyst walked next to the bed, and her sad eyes locked on Emma.

"The witch is dead." We all had to be losing our minds since we couldn't figure out what was going on.

"I know. That's what is so perplexing." Beatrice sighed and glanced around the room.

"Aidan, why don't you go get something to eat while I stay here with Emma." Amethyst smiled and reached over Emma, placing a hand on my shoulder. "You haven't eaten in over a day."

"No, I can't eat or sleep." There was no way I was leaving her side. I'd be right here until she woke up again.

Emma

I STILL FELT like I was falling, but I had no clue where to. Endora had made it sound like I'd be hunting for the missing clue, but it seemed like hours had passed since we'd spoken. At some point, I'd have to stop falling, right?

The air gradually warmed, which should have been comforting, but what if this was some demented game and I wound up in Hell?

"Aidan, you have to take care of yourself or you won't be able to help her." Amethyst's voice reached my ears. It was the most beautiful voice I'd ever heard.

"How can I do that when she's like this?" Aidan's voice broke, and my heart fractured.

Our bond connected again, and his anxiety and hurt flowed through me.

"Emma?" Hope filled his voice as he felt our connection reopen. He shifted beside me, rising to see my face.

Yes. I still hadn't hit solid ground, so it was the only way I could respond.

"I can hear her." Aidan placed his hands on my shoulders, and I realized I was back home.

It took a second, but before long, I opened my eyes.

"Oh, thank goddess," Beatrice cried as she ran over to stand next to Amethyst. All three of them stared down at me.

This was awkward as sin. "Uh ... hey." I met each one of their gazes before my eyes stayed on Aidan's. I'd never seen him so broken.

He pulled me back into his arms and hugged me hard. "I thought I'd lost you."

I'd been scared for myself, so I could only imagine how he'd felt. "I'm sorry."

"What happened?" Amethyst asked.

The last thing I wanted to do was get out of this bed. Aidan was a wreck of emotions, but they all needed to hear what I'd learned. *Can we go talk with the others and then come back here, just you and me?*

Yes, as long as you stay beside me. Aidan nodded and loosened his hold on me.

"Is everyone around?" It would take a minute or two for them to all gather.

"Yeah. Everyone is in the den." Amethyst straightened and headed for the door. "Should I tell Finn to leave?"

"Yeah, he doesn't need to hear what I have to say."

"On it." She frowned and exited the room.

I took in a deep breath and climbed out of bed. "I'm surprised everyone is still here. I figured Gabby and Logan would have bailed."

"Dear girl, they respect you more than they let on. No one has left this house since you ..." Beatrice paused, contemplating her next words. "... passed out?"

"Yeah, I can't help you there." It had been insane. "I'm not sure what it was either, but it doesn't matter. I'm back now." I headed out the door, ready to tell everyone what had happened.

"So, you met the original witch, and she's your ancestor?" Beth's eyes widened as she took it all in. She sat in the middle of the couch, between Ada and Honor.

I stood in the middle of the den in front of the fireplace, and all fifteen pairs of eyes were on me. Beatrice sat in the recliner on my left with Amethyst standing behind her, while Sage sat in the recliner on my right, with Samuel behind her. The other witches stood behind the couch, and the remainder of the shifter group sat on the ground.

I should've probably sat down, but I was extremely restless. Apparently, I'd been gone for over a day, so I guessed I had a lot of pent-up energy. "Yes, and it's crazy."

"But she's dead." Gabby's cold words filled the room. "That doesn't make any sense."

"When a witch dies, they become part of nature since magic never truly ceases to exist." I was still coming to grips with this too. Maybe all of these haunted houses were real. It could be the leftover magic of witches guarding their homes or secrets.

"That's what older witches believed, but that thought had died out with the advent of modern medicines and science." Beatrice crossed her legs and leaned back in the recliner. "Which proves that some knowledge gets lost or altered after time."

"So, what's our next step?" Samuel asked as everyone looked at me for guidance.

They expected me to have answers, and the problem was I had none. *I don't know what to do.* I needed my anchor.

Go with your gut. Aidan stepped closer to my side and took my hand, supporting me.

"Well, she said there is a piece of the puzzle that can be found with each girl." We had to figure out what she meant to move forward.

"We combined your blood, and that didn't work." Rowan paced behind the couch, her pacing under the lights making her red hair seem more orange. "So ... what else could it be?"

She was right. If the puzzle piece was found with each girl, you'd think it would be blood-related, especially considering how important blood was for witchcraft. We had to be overlooking something.

"What about your marks?" Aidan moved my hair to the

side and looked at my full pentagram birthmark behind my left ear. "That mark is important. Could it be something in there?"

"He's on to something." Coral glanced at Gabby. "Yours is the top-right vertex, right?"

"Yeah." Gabby nodded. "We all know that."

"Stop with the attitude." I wasn't in the mood. "Otherwise, you can leave."

Her eyes widened at the annoyance in my voice, but she remained silent and sitting.

"Oh, my God," Ivory breathed. "We're missing the top vertex."

I scanned each girl, thinking of their mark. "You're right. I thought it was meant for me since I have the whole star, but what if there is another girl."

"But how do we confirm that?" Sunny blinked as she tried catching up with everything, seeing as she was the newest addition with the least amount of experience.

"With the map." Honor chuckled like we had it figured out. "Amethyst, do you know where it is?"

Amethyst took off toward her room. "Of course. I'll be right back."

The more I thought about it, the more I was certain that was the missing piece. *Aidan, if this proves to be right, the original witch warned me not to trust her at first. That each drop of her blood has its demons.* I didn't want to be that transparent with the group of girls before me, but Aidan needed to be in the same place as me. *There's no telling where we'll find her.*

It doesn't matter. He wrapped an arm around my waist and kissed my cheek. *We'll figure it out together.*

Amethyst's footsteps hurried back down the hallway,

and I tensed. For all I knew, we might have to drive back to California, which would suck huge monkey balls.

She placed the map on the coffee table. Each marked girl stood over the map.

"It's just like what we did with the witch's diary but on the map instead." I smiled at Sunny, hoping to ease her nerves.

"Okay." She stared at the map, concern still showing on her face, but she nodded.

Like every other time, we dropped our blood in order, from me and the clockwise vertices. We were all here in Columbus, so that's where each drop of blood crawled to. However, when Sunny mixed her blood with ours, it inched northeast and stopped at Athens, Georgia.

"There is another girl." Gabby sucked in a breath, disbelief lacing each word. "I thought this would lead to a dead end."

"So, there are six girls." My mind began racing like crazy. "I'm technically not one of the sides ... I'm the center that caused the star to rise." Why hadn't we figured that out together?

Coral laughed without mirth. "The Hallowed Guild was never supposed to know the true number of girls, and the witches assumed it was five."

"Then, we need to go get her." That was our only option.

"It's only three hours from here." Beth stood, ready to go.

"No, we leave tomorrow." Aidan met my gaze. "You've been out for twenty-four hours with no food or rest."

"You just said I'd been out—"

"It wasn't rest, and we both know it." Aidan arched an eyebrow, daring me to contradict him.

Even though I hated to admit it, I was exhausted. I glanced at the clock on the wall and realized it was already seven in the evening. "Fine, but we leave first thing."

"That's fair. We'll get there early enough to get a room." Remus motioned around the house. "It's safer to be here than out there. Maybe we can even get there and get back in a day."

"It would be ideal." We were safest here under the coven's protection. "Let's go grab something to eat and get to bed early."

AFTER EATING, I took a quick shower and headed back into the bedroom. Aidan was already lying there, and his honey eyes met mine.

"Joining me?" He held his arms out wide for me to crawl into.

I was happy to oblige. I settled against his chest, and he pulled back so our eyes met. "I was so damn scared."

"I'm sorry. I tried connecting with you, but she had my wolf blocked." I never wanted to go back to that place again. It was scary as hell. "It was dark, cold, and lonely."

"You don't have anything to apologize for." He tucked a piece of stray hair behind my ear. "I'm just so glad you're back here safe and sound." His lips lowered to mine, and his minty taste soothed a part of my soul I hadn't even realized needed it.

I deepened the kiss. I needed him and to feel him inside me. I needed to know I was back here and alive.

My hand went to his boxers, and I tugged them off his hips. Not missing a beat, I pulled back and yanked his shirt over his head.

Hey, we can go slow. His words were comforting in my head.

No, not tonight. Not waiting for him to remove my clothes, I stripped before my lips connected back with his, and I rolled him over.

As I straddled him, he lifted, pulling a nipple inside his mouth and flicking it with his tongue. He wanted to have foreplay, but not tonight. I didn't need it.

I guided him inside me, and he groaned in ecstasy. I moved on top of him, and his hips thrust in tune with my body.

I grabbed the headboard, using it to steady myself. He bit gently at my nipple then pulled away and scooted closer to the headboard.

The friction built, and I spread my legs farther apart, needing him to hit deeper ... to be deeper.

Our pleasure collided, bringing us both closer to the edge.

His hands gripped my hips, his fingers digging into my waist. He guided me to move faster and pounded into me, and an orgasm took hold. We rode as bliss consumed our bodies and bond.

When it was all over, I landed on my side and into his arms. Tonight, I was happy and safe. Who knew what tomorrow would bring?

CHAPTER FIVE

The next morning, our group began our journey early. The same thirteen of us took off in the two Suburbans, heading to Athens.

I wasn't sure what to expect. Each girl was different from one another and had been harder and harder to bring home. I was assuming that was part of the worthiness test included in the curse ... prophecy. I still hadn't sorted out what I considered this unwanted birthright that fate had bestowed upon me to be.

Samuel drove the other car with the witches, Beth, Sunny, Ada, and Honor as usual while the rest of us rode in the vehicle Aidan was driving.

"Do we have a plan?" Gabby asked from the backseat. She had her back leaned against the driver's side of the Suburban with her legs in Logan's lap.

"Nope. Not yet." They expected me to know more than I did. Yes, I'd met with Endora, but she hadn't given me any real information, only clues and riddles. "You know as much as I do."

"At least, she gave you the right hint to figure out we were missing a girl," Ivory stated.

I turned my head to look at her over my shoulder. She was also sitting on the driver's side, except she was in the middle row, making her the easiest to see out of everyone. I hadn't spent much time with her—or any one of the girls, really—but I already felt a kinship with her. She was warm, supportive, and in many ways reminded me of Amethyst, just a tad more timid. Her mate was similar, and I loved just how damn devoted they were to each other.

"Which you'd think a good leader could have figured out themselves," Logan mumbled, but his words were clear as day to my ears.

That was the point.

Aidan's hands tightened on the steering wheel, but if he fought this battle for me, I would look weak.

I turned fully in my seat and met Logan's eyes dead-on. "I didn't see you figuring it out, so I guess that means you're pretty worthless yourself."

His light eyes glowed. "But I'm not the destined—"

"Are you sure about that?" I hated that he was so egotistical and ready to point out anything negative. "I mean ... take a look. So far, three out of the six girls have a mate tied to The Hallowed Guild. Doesn't that seem perplexing?"

Logan's brow furrowed as he tried to follow my train of thought. "What does that have to do with anything?"

Remus's dark green eyes lightened slightly. "It's as if the witch is making sure both witch and shifter stand side by side."

"And the shifter is tied to the original alpha through The Hallowed Guild." Aidan took my hand. "I hadn't even considered that."

"Which means you were all chosen to lead and are just

as much part of the story as the women." I lifted an eyebrow at the brooding alpha. "We're all leaders, not just me. Endora is only counting on me to fulfill her dream, but you are all leaders beside me. This isn't me against you. We need to work as a team. If the vertices haven't proved that, then I'm guessing you're not up for the challenge."

Logan frowned, and Gabby narrowed her bright blue eyes at me. She tilted her head, taking in my words.

The rest of the car ride continued in silence.

I'm pretty sure this is Prescott's pack we're visiting. Aidan's jaw tightened.

Why do you say that? This caught me off guard. I hadn't expected to face that pack again and had pushed them out of my mind, which seemed foolish now.

Because my dad visited them after he'd told me I would be attending Crawford University. Prescott was going to the University of Georgia close by but transferred to Crawford.

That meant we were going to face an enemy we'd already fought.

How should we handle this? Aidan asked with concern.

We'll warn the others and go in. There weren't many other options. *We stay the course.*

Okay. He nodded as he took a right turn on the highway.

Maybe she won't be with them. Some of the other covens had been protecting the girls. Maybe it was all just a moot point.

You're right. He sucked in a breath, and his shoulders relaxed a little.

There's no point in stressing out until we get there. I took a calming breath.

The closer we got, the more tension built in the vehicle. If this foreshadowed what we were coming up against, I worried whether we could find this girl. For this to be the last girl to prove our worth, that had to say something ... something I was trying hard not to focus on.

We rolled into the college town a little after eleven, and we followed Samuel to a restaurant with parking available on the road.

As I climbed out of the vehicle, Beth walked over and took my hand. "I Googled restaurants, and this diner is supposed to have huge hamburgers at decent prices."

My stomach growled. "Sounds good to me."

Our large group entered the diner through the red door. Oval tables were scattered across the black and white checkered floor, and tables with booth seating on one side and chairs on the other lined the wall. A bar was front and center of the small restaurant.

There wasn't a big lunchtime crowd, but three tables were already occupied.

A man in his mid-twenties made his way over to us, and the musky scent of wolf hit me hard right in the chest. "Hey, how many are in your party?"

He must have smelled the same thing from us because he raised an eyebrow.

"Thirteen." I forced the word out, portraying a level of confidence I didn't really have. My mother's words from so long ago, when I'd started school and felt like I didn't fit in there or in my pack, repeated in my head: "Fake it. If you pretend long enough, you'll start believing it."

I'd never told her that it didn't work ... at least, not for me. However, it did with the others, and I'd learned that was enough.

"Let me pull together a few tables in the back corner." He turned and headed to the back corner to make room for us.

I linked with Aidan. *He's a wolf.*

Yeah, this can't be good. He ran his fingers through my hair, ensuring my mark was covered. *We need to be careful with the others, too.*

That wouldn't be possible here with wolfman. He'd overhear. "Hey, ladies. I forgot something in the car. Do you mind coming with me?"

Beth narrowed her eyes but nodded. "Sure, let's go."

Our group of girls headed outside, and I walked to the Suburbans, not wanting to look suspicious. When we reached them, I opened the passenger door and pretended to look for something. I whispered, "That guy might be part of the local Hallowed Guild pack, so we need to cover our marks."

Ivory frowned. "Wait ... there's a pack here? That's not good."

"No, it's not, but it is what it is. Let's eat and then drive around until we feel the tug, but we must be cautious." I lifted my purse. "Found it," I said loudly in case anyone was around to overhear.

"Yeah, okay." Beth snorted and waved us back in. "Let's eat before I get hangry."

Aidan

"Is EVERYTHING OKAY?" The server glanced out the window at the girls. His shaggy, golden-brown hair fell over his forehead, only giving a peek of his caramel eyes.

"Yeah, you know how women are." If he thought he would get something from me, he was greatly mistaken. "They travel in packs." I'd chosen that last word on purpose.

"That I understand." The waiter stared at me. "You look familiar."

Here I was, worried about the girls' marks when I should've been more concerned with my face. "No clue how." I shrugged, forcing the mask of indifference to stay on my face. "I'm not from around here."

"Which brings me to another point. Have you informed my ..." He paused and chewed his bottom lip. "... boss that you're here?"

Ah, he'd almost said *alpha* in front of humans. That would have raised questions. "No. We're just passing through."

"Does he require notice in those situations as well?" Remus sat at the far end of the table.

I sat down right in front of him with Samuel taking the other end.

"We like to make sure we know who is here." The server pulled out his phone. "I'll give him a call and be right back to take your orders." He paused and stared straight into Samuel's eyes before walking away.

My shoulders tensed with each step he took. "This is bad." I lowered my voice so the humans and the server wouldn't hear. "He's already noted Samuel. When the other two come in ..." I didn't even know how to finish that sentence.

Logan plopped down two seats away from Remus. "But if we leave now, it'll be suspicious."

That was putting it mildly. "We stay and eat." Unless he told us otherwise.

Emma

WE ENTERED THE RESTAURANT, and I made a beeline to Aidan and took my seat next to him. *Is everything okay?*

No, the server is calling The Hallowed Guild alpha to inform him that we're here. Also, he noticed that Samuel is a witch.

What? How? I picked up a menu and scanned it, making sure my body wasn't too rigid. The last thing we needed was to put ourselves on the pack's radar.

Because they want to vet visitors. He took my hand in his. *But don't worry, I won't allow anything to happen to you.*

I bit my tongue to prevent the real words I wanted to say to him from coming out. The truth was he couldn't protect me. My trip to purgatory had taught us both that. *Did he say something to Samuel?*

Surprisingly, no. Aidan nibbled on his bottom lip. *But I don't know if that's good or bad.*

Either way, we're stuck. Leaving would only make it worse. *Logan is right. It would look odd if we left.*

Agreed.

"Ohhh ..." Beth sat next to me and pointed right at the double bacon cheeseburger. "It'll be fun putting that into my belly."

The server returned and stopped cold a few steps away from our table. "Interesting company you all keep." The man pulled out his notepad and pen.

The table a couple of feet away stopped drinking and turned in our direction.

"I'm sorry?" It had to be the witches. As part of the secret society, he would hate them. However, I couldn't believe he'd made such a blatant comment here.

"Nothing, forget it." The man smiled, but the rest of his expression remained dark.

"Why don't we relocate you outside?" The server's jaw clenched as he took in a breath. "It might be more comfortable for all of you."

"Sure, that would be nice." That way we could talk without worrying about him overhearing.

Our group stood and made our way outside.

"Here, let me push together some tables." The server diligently worked, and soon, we had a similar setup to what we had inside.

We sat down in the same order, and the wind picked up, stirring my hair.

I held it in place.

We ordered our food, and the wolf went back inside to fill the orders.

"We need to get the hell out of here." Coral tapped her finger against the metal table. "He's not happy about our presence here."

"No." I wanted to do the same thing, but if we ran, they'd want to know why. They were already suspicious, and adding in the witches put a target on our backs.

"We just need to wait," Remus agreed. "The more we appear like we don't want to meet them, the worse it will be."

"It doesn't matter." We were on the defensive. If the witches disappear now, it'll look like we know they have a problem with them."

Samuel ran a hand down his face. "This is fucking crazy."

Something inside nudged me, as if in warning. I lifted my finger to my lips, alerting the others.

Do you smell something? Aidan sniffed.

No, but something is off. Maybe we were being watched. *We need to act normal.*

"I'm starving." I put the menus in the holder in the center of the table and rubbed my stomach.

"Girl, I'm ready for that meat." Beth licked her lips.

"You have a knack for making things sound perverted." Coral laughed. "Don't ever change."

"Oh, I don't plan to." Beth winked.

"I don't understand how anyone could be friends with people who don't eat meat." Sunny shook her head. She'd been shocked when she'd learned that the witches were vegetarians.

"That's one way of putting it." A deep voice sounded from behind us. "In fact, you shouldn't be friends."

I spun around and stared into the eyes of a man who looked like an older version of Prescott.

CHAPTER SIX

"So ... what do we have here?" The older man joined us on the patio and sat in a chair close to Amethyst and Coral, which made my skin crawl. His hair was slightly darker than Prescott's light brown, and the alpha's eyes were black, much like his soul. He adjusted his jeans, causing his black shirt to crinkle.

"A group of friends trying to enjoy lunch." If he wanted to play a game, so be it.

"Well, the shifters I don't mind, but there are three of you I'd rather see leave immediately," he replied hatefully.

"We're a package deal." I wouldn't let him talk down to my friends.

"Yes, I see that." He laced his fingers together in front of his body. "Have we met before?"

Aidan linked with me, and his body stiffened beside me. *He's goading us.*

Then, we have to be smarter. At least I hoped I could be. "Nope, but we get that a lot." I forced a smile, suggesting I wasn't concerned. "But with a group of college kids like ours, I'm sure it's hard to tell us all apart."

He tapped his pointer finger against his hand. "I'm certain that's not it."

If he wanted to force me into admitting something, he would be grossly disappointed. "Hmm, I'm not seeing it."

Gabby batted her eyelashes. "I'm not even from this area, so I have to say you've been misinformed."

"Oh, really now." His face lit up. "Where are you from?"

She needs to stop talking. Aidan cleared his throat, diverting the alpha's attention to him. "They're family friends here visiting."

The fact that the stench of a lie didn't fill the air surprised me. He actually thought of them as family.

"You consider these witches family?" The alpha shifted his weight, leaning toward us.

Warning filled my body with its cold tendrils.

"Why? Is that not acceptable?" Aidan rubbed his chin.

We were playing a dangerous game here in front of every human that might be watching.

"Of course it isn't." The alpha's eyes glowed faintly. "I would expect a Murphy to know that."

There it was. There was no playing anymore. He knew.

"Well, you have your facts wrong. I'm not a Murphy." Aidan lifted an eyebrow, and once again, the stench of a lie was absent. *They disowned me, after all.*

I hated that they had, but it was working in our favor. I wanted to apologize again, but it was futile. I hadn't forced his hand; his father had when they'd attacked the coven for protecting us.

"Interesting." The alpha tapped his fingers on the table. "You see, a coven and some shifters attacked us. I wasn't there, but there is some sort of vengeance that needs to be had."

It took everything inside me not to correct him. We hadn't attacked them; they'd attacked us. But if I corrected him, that would confirm we'd been there. Right now, he was fishing.

Coral's face turned pink in anger.

I decided to act fast before she blurted something incriminating and he declared war on us right then and there. "Well, I understand why you'd feel that way. I hope you find who you're looking for."

"Oh, we will." The alpha straightened his shoulders. "You see, when we find the missing Murphy kid, it'll make things come full circle."

He can't prove it's you. The alpha had nothing to go on.

He placed his hand on my thigh. *Yeah, I bet my dad is kicking himself tonight, but you're worth it.*

Good. I'd hate for you to resent me for it. There it was, my big fear. I never wanted him to regret choosing me.

Never. I only wish I'd made the decision sooner. He squeezed my hand. *We wasted four years.*

No, it made us who we needed to be to survive. I didn't like to admit it, but after meeting Endora and hearing her story, it was true. We hadn't been strong enough to fulfill an ancient prophecy and take on a secret society at fourteen. We'd required years to grow into the strong shifters we were today. "I'm sure everything will work out." The words were hard to speak, but we had to reduce his suspicion as much as possible.

"Me too." He stood. "Maybe the wolf shifters would like to join our pack for dinner? It's not often we get visitors."

If we said no, it would cause problems. I surveyed our group, and Ivory nodded, confirming what I already suspected. We had to say yes. "Sure, but not all of my friends are invited?"

Annoyance lined his face. "It's in their best interest if they aren't in attendance."

They're trying to separate us. Aidan nodded. "We'll be there."

"Perfect. Be there at sundown." He turned and headed to leave. "Do you need directions?"

It was a test. "No, we're good. We'll see you then." I purposely turned my attention back to the table, dismissing him.

Aidan chuckled. *He hates that he mainly talked to you. He doesn't like that you're the leader of our little group.*

That sounded about right. *Eh, he'll get over it.*

Once he'd driven off, I blew out a breath. "This will be fun."

"I guess we won't be making it home tonight," Samuel pouted.

"Actually, you three need to." It wasn't safe for them here, especially since the pack knew they were witches. "He wants to separate us."

"You need both vehicles, though." Amethyst sipped her water.

"That's what rentals are for." Beth pointed at me. "Am I right?"

Lord knew I needed that smile right now. "Yes, ma'am. You are."

"That works," Coral said. "I feel like we're abandoning you, though. You could be walking into a trap."

"Maybe ... possibly ... But you guys can come back tomorrow." We didn't have much of a choice. We needed to find that girl, and for all we knew, The Hallowed Guild pack had her. "I can give Jacob a call and get a feel for where Prescott is."

"No, that would be too suspicious," Aidan growled.

He was right. *I'm sorry. I wasn't thinking about your feelings.*

No, you're mine. I need to calm down over it, but it really would be too suspicious.

"Maybe call your parents," Beth suggested. "It's been a few days anyway. They could know something. After all, Prescott jumped Jacob."

I hadn't even considered that avenue, and my parents would appreciate a call.

The outside porch door opened, and the server carried out the group's food. Now we needed to eat and stop talking due to prying ears.

———

OUR GROUP GOT SITUATED in a Holiday Inn Express, and we left the marked wolves and their friends behind as Aidan, Beth, and I drove the witches to a rental place nearby.

"Are you sure this is the best decision?" Amethyst shifted in her seat, clearly not happy with them splitting from our group.

"No, I'm not." She already knew how I felt, which was why she was pushing the issue. "But if you stay, things could take a turn for the worse, and we have to find the girl. This is the best option, even if it isn't ideal."

"She's right." Aidan glanced in the rearview mirror. "But if you don't want to go all the way back to Columbus, you can find a hotel and stay the night thirty minutes away from here. That way, you'll be close, but if they track down our hotel, you won't be there."

"That I can work with." Coral stared out her window as we pulled into a car rental place. "I was going to talk

Amethyst into not going far anyway. You all may need us."

"And that's why we get along so well," Beth snorted. "Because had I been in your shoes, I'd have done the same thing."

"Yeah, we'll be close by," Samuel grumbled from the very backseat. "We're in this together."

For them to fight to stay by our side proved that even if we weren't blood relatives, we were truly a family. "Okay, but you need to stay put and not venture out. A wolf from their pack could work nearby since it's not far away. The last thing we need is for a wolf to see you and call Prescott or his father."

"We can order pizza or something for dinner." Amethyst grabbed her red purse from the footwell.

Aidan pulled into a parking spot. "Sounds like a plan. We'll call you when we get back to our hotel for the night."

"We need to get moving in case someone is following us." I hated leaving them alone, but the sooner they put distance between us, the better.

"No, it's fine." Amethyst opened the door. "We'll text you once we're settled in."

Within minutes, our vehicle was pulling out of the parking lot, and Aidan turned the Suburban back toward the hotel to meet with the others.

"I should probably call Mom." I pulled my phone from my pocket and dialed her number. Like always, she answered by the second ring.

"Emma?" Her hopeful voice filled my ear.

"Hey, Mom." It'd been a few days since I'd called her. "How are you?"

"Worried sick about you. It's been weeks since you called." She sounded hurt.

Oh, damn. I'd thought it had only been days. "I'm sorry. It's been a little crazy. We're doing okay."

"Good. Do you think you can come home soon?"

"I'm not sure. I hope so." This situation wasn't ideal. "How's Jacob doing?"

"Surprisingly well." Her tone turned cold. "He forgave his roommate, which was asinine of him. I'd thought he was smart, but it doesn't matter. He's not my worry right now. Apparently, he has a game several hours away. I think in Kentucky this weekend."

Okay, that was good news. They wouldn't be near us. *The last pack that attacked us was your father's, right?*

Yeah. Aidan sighed. *It was my former pack, but either way, they couldn't really see us since we were in the car when they came through. Most of them were in the woods, so this pack could've been involved too. As long as they don't link me to Dad's pack, we should be fine.*

"You and Dad are staying close to the pack and not leaving, right?" I didn't want the Murphy pack to get a hold of them and use them against me. They were my main weakness, outside of Aidan.

"Yes, we've been staying at home." She chuckled. "I could get used to people getting my groceries for me."

She'd always despised going to the grocery store, so she wasn't kidding. "Well, I'm glad I could help you there."

"No, I'd rather have you here with me." A small sob escaped her.

And this was why I'd put off calling her. It made the whole situation worse, but I hated hearing her like this. "I miss you too." I meant every single word. "I promise to call more often."

"Please do." She sniffed. "I love you, baby girl."

"I love you too." I pulled the phone away from my face. "Bye." Then, I pressed END.

"At least we don't have to worry about the dumbass being there tonight." Beth sank into her seat and closed her eyes. "At some point, we'll actually be able to rest again, right?"

"I'm sorry I dragged you into this." Her being my roommate back at the university had become a major disadvantage for her.

"Girl, this is the most exciting thing that's ever happened in my life." Beth yawned and stretched her arms over her head. "Don't you dare apologize for it."

She did like to be involved in the drama.

We pulled into the Holiday Inn parking lot, and within minutes, we were walking into our room where everyone else was.

Ada and Honor had taken one of the queen-sized beds, with Sunny, Gabby, and Ivory sitting on the other. Ivory sat on the edge, leaning against Remus's chest while he rubbed her shoulders. Logan sat in the small desk chair. The desk was right next to the television, and they had it turned so everyone could see.

The thin carpet, with its large alternating squares of neutral colors, was the same as in any cheap hotel room. A white comforter was on each bed, with a wooden headboard, and a box platform beneath it. Between the beds was a small wooden end table that held two lamps and a phone.

"Are they heading back home?" Remus asked, removing his hands from Ivory's shoulders.

"Slight change of plans." I joined Ada and Honor on the bed and noticed the makeup and brushes laying on the comforter. "They're going thirty minutes east in case something happens and we need backup."

"Three witches can be adequate backup?" Logan rolled the chair around to face me.

"Yeah, especially if the pack isn't expecting them." They could hold their own. "They didn't get hurt in the last attack."

"I guess that's something." Gabby shrugged. "It's getting late. We should begin tracking them."

"Let's cover up Emma's mark too." Honor turned her head and pointed to her unblemished skin. "We figured we needed to use some concealer to hide the mark in case our hair moved out of the way."

"Smart woman." I turned and moved my hair to the side so she could work on me.

"Emma and I need to go by different names." Aidan scratched his nose. "The alpha knows my dad and brother."

"What should we call you?" Beth's shoulders shook with laughter. "Romeo and Juliet?"

"How about James and Angel?" Aidan suggested. "Dad called me my middle name, James, from time to time, and Angel is one of her nicknames. That way it's not a lie."

"Yeah, fine." Logan flipped through his phone, disinterested.

Honor dropped her brushes and smiled. "Done."

"Good, we shouldn't be late." I'd wanted to rest for a few minutes before leaving, but we had no clue where to find them, and I was hoping we'd find the girl on our way.

Why are they in our room? Aidan frowned, his gaze catching mine.

Remember, it's Beth's room too, and they're hanging out. We should be happy. The more time they spent with one another, the more they'd be invested in the cause. We all needed to be friends.

I guess you're right, but they could've done it in their

room. Aidan intertwined his fingers with mine. *Beth is a handful on her own, let alone the entire group.*

They were waiting on us. Maybe all of this would work out after all. Even Gabby and Logan weren't being as combative. "You guys ready?"

Sunny jumped to her feet and grinned. "Yeah, let's do this."

I wished I shared her enthusiasm, but I couldn't help but feel we were walking into a trap. They had something up their sleeves, and it wouldn't take us long to figure out what.

CHAPTER SEVEN

W e piled into the two vehicles with Beth driving the other Suburban. The single ladies had taken that vehicle while the fated couples rode with Aidan and me.

Any idea which direction we should go? Aidan pulled onto the road from the parking lot.

Not really. I didn't feel the tug yet, but we had a bigger fish to fry. *Let's head to the woods.* I pointed to the part of town we hadn't ventured into yet.

Ivory rolled down the passenger window in the middle row. "Let's see if we can pick up any scents as we drive by."

Great idea. Remus, Aidan, and I followed her lead.

Gabby glared at the windows. "We can't roll the windows down back here."

"It's not a big deal. There's enough wind blowing through the car that we'll be able to pick something up too." Logan wrapped an arm around Gabby and pulled her close.

They weren't being ornery ... yet. We drove through the quaint, beautiful town. The leaves were changing colors, and people milled about in the streets, their bulky jackets keeping out the chill. Older but well-maintained brick buildings made up most of the town.

"Do we know what to expect?" Remus kept his attention glued on the people we were passing.

"Not really." I doubted they'd do something when we first got there. My gut told me this was an expedition meeting. "We should be okay, but we need to be on guard. Since we were with witches, they'll be watching everything we do."

Ivory bit her lip. "It would be really helpful if we had a pack link so we could communicate amongst each other."

"But to do that, we'd have to choose an alpha." I agreed with her but choosing an alpha could be tricky. I didn't want us to be at each other's throats.

"That's no problem for me." Ivory placed a hand on my shoulder. "I already view you as our leader."

Her words felt heavy on my shoulders. I didn't want them to think I was pressuring them to choose me. "Thank you, but if we decide to go that route, we'll need to all be in agreement with who the alpha is."

"Ivory is right, though. It should be you." Remus was on the same page as his mate.

Gabby fell back against the chair and frowned. "Just because she found us doesn't mean she should be the one."

And this proved my point.

"You think you should be the alpha?" Ivory turned, glaring at the wolf shifter. "You're angry and, dare I say, combative just for the fun of it."

Ivory's reaction shocked me. Her demeanor reminded me so much of Amethyst—warm, kind, and loving.

Logan blinked. "What happened to the meek girl back at the hotel?"

Something pulled at me unexpectedly and took my breath away. "I feel her."

"Which way do I go?" Aidan clutched the steering wheel.

"Stay on course." This was the strongest tug out of all of them.

"It's almost hard to breathe." Gabby rasped and slumped against Logan.

That described it perfectly. The tug filled me so much that it felt like my lungs didn't have room to expand.

I sagged against the car door, attempting to stay upright, and grasped the door handle to ground myself.

My phone rang over and over again, but I couldn't answer it. I was at the mercy of the connection to the last girl. The call ended, only for Aidan's phone to begin ringing instead.

It had to be Beth.

Aidan had the Suburban's Bluetooth answer it. "Hey."

"So, I have two marked wolves spazzing out in my car," Beth said with concern. "I'm assuming you do too since Emma didn't answer her phone."

"I'm not sure *spazzing* is the right word, but I have three wolves who feel the tug to the last girl, and it seems stronger than before." Aidan glanced at me out of the corner of his eye, concern etched into his face.

"Same thing," Beth said, dismissing his correction. "I'm following you but wanted to make sure they all were feeling it and not just these two wimps."

Ada snorted so loud we heard it over the phone.

"You are something," Aidan sighed.

"Aw, thanks," Beth cooed.

"He didn't mean it as a compliment." I'd have to give her hell even if I felt like I was being ripped in two.

"At least, she's not too out of it." A loud moan from Beth's car interrupted the conversation. "I guess I better go. See you guys soon."

That sounded like it could've been Sunny, which worried me even more. Of all of the girls we'd found, she'd been injured the worst.

We were rolling out of the town, and the trees were thickening. The tugging sensation was pulling me to go right. "Turn right on the next road."

"Okay." Aidan slammed on the brakes and cut the wheel to the right, putting us into the left lane and oncoming traffic.

A loud honk blared as a car in the other lane headed straight at us.

I sucked in a breath and braced myself for the hit.

"Fuck me." Aidan spun the wheel hard, and the back end of our vehicle fishtailed, narrowly missing the oncoming car.

Aidan straightened the wheel, and we turned onto the road that headed in the direction I'd told him to go.

"Holy shit," Remus groaned from the back. "I think I might puke." He hung his head out the window.

If Samuel had been here, he'd be making dog jokes. Actually, some humor would do us some good.

"I know you didn't know until you told me, but some advanced warning would be nice." Aidan took my hand and squeezed it gently.

"I can't make any promises." The tug wasn't an exact science.

He slowed the vehicle as we began passing several back roads. "I figured, but we shouldn't have the same problem now."

Yeah, the speed limit was lower here.

The farther we drove, the more discomfort pulled at me. "We're heading the right way." I closed my eyes and focused on breathing. It was getting to be difficult. A warning laced the tug; that's why it overpowered me. It echoed Endora's words from my subconscious or whatever it was.

"I smell wolves," Logan said from the backseat. "We're getting close."

"Maybe we should find a place to park and go the rest of the way on foot." It wouldn't be smart to take our vehicles there.

"We can scope things out easier that way." Aidan nodded. "There's a park up ahead. We can leave our vehicles there."

My eyes fell on a Sandy Creek Park sign. "That's perfect." The woods abutted the park, so it would be a good place to start.

A few minutes later, we were parked and heading toward the woods. The sun was close to setting.

Without the witches, we could move faster and still be silent. A small group of college kids was hanging out at the campgrounds, surrounding a firepit. I'd always imagined that would be me, but no. Here I was fighting for my life.

Our group stepped into the woods, and soon, we were away from anything that smelled human. I hurried to the front to lead with the marked girls right behind.

"The tug is following the wolves' scents." We were heading toward a pack that believed in the curse and were actively trying to kill us, so if she's with them, it couldn't be a good thing.

If you see anything out of the ordinary, let me know immediately. Aidan's concern coursed through our bond.

Promise. We passed by trees, and animals scurried around us. At least, nothing too horrible happened here where the animals had left. Silence would have been a bad omen.

The sky glowed with pinks, purples, and blues as the sun set. We reached thinning trees. *We're almost there.* The tug eased when a neighborhood came into view. It was set up like most pack homes: remote, surrounded by woods, and with immaculate houses. There had to be at least twenty-five, which meant it was a decent-sized pack.

As soon as I stepped out of the woods and into someone's backyard, two pack shifters appeared in front of me with their arms crossed. They looked to be in their thirties and rugged.

"Who are you?" The taller one had two inches on me and dropped his arms to his sides. His glass-green eyes focused on me, and the breeze blew his short cherry-brown hair.

"Your alpha invited us to dinner here." If they were trying to intimidate me, they'd learn a huge lesson.

"Aw, you think you're the leader, don't you?" The shifter that was my height lifted a bronze eyebrow that matched his man bun. He was thicker than the other one but had nothing on Aidan.

"She is our leader." Aidan stepped beside me and stared them down. "Do you have a problem with that?"

"Females aren't meant to lead." The shorter one wrinkled his nose in disgust. "They don't have the chops to do what it takes."

The back door to the house opened, and the alpha stepped out. "Asher, stand down."

The shorter guy turned to face the alpha. "These are the wolves you invited?"

"Yes, so they are our guests," he replied sternly, "and we will treat them as such."

The taller guy glanced at me and back to his leader. "But they have a woman as their—"

"They are our guests," the alpha growled. "Don't make me say it again."

"No, it's good that they're so protective." I needed to diffuse the situation. "You can never be too careful."

"There are no truer words than those." The alpha closed the distance between us and held his hand out toward me. "I realize I never gave you my name. It's Barry."

I didn't want to touch his hand, but that wasn't a feasible option. I was determined to at least pretend to be polite. When my skin touched his, a coldness skittered down my back. It felt exactly like the warning I felt on our way over. *He's dangerous.*

Aidan held his hand out, making Barry release my hand to shake his. *How so?*

I don't know. It's just a feeling. I didn't know how to explain it any better. The tug was still there, but the warning was connected to the man standing in front of us. I was sure he was involved in The Hallowed Guild, and I would bet money on how.

"So, you two are mates." He tipped his head to the side. "That makes sense."

"I'm James." Aidan dropped the alpha's hand and placed his arm around my waist. "And this is Angel."

"It's very nice to meet you all." Barry pointed to the rest of the group. "And you are?"

They introduced themselves, although Sunny hung back a little. She was the most skittish among us.

"Well, the food should be almost finished." He waved at us to follow him. "Come meet the others."

Now that he'd mentioned it, the smell of steak was thick in the air. My stomach growled so loudly everyone heard it.

"Hungry, Angel?" Beth snickered from behind.

"Oh, bite me." It was important for us to act normal, and our banter made this whole situation bearable.

"James would get jealous," Beth sighed dramatically. "Otherwise, I'd be down."

"Are those two always like that?" Barry asked.

"Sometimes worse." Aidan chuckled. "They're behaving for you." *Stay beside me the entire night. I don't trust him.*

Don't worry. I don't plan to run astray. I looped my arm through his, anchoring myself to him.

The neighborhood consisted of older homes similar to the housing in Mount Juliet. The homes were probably at least fifty to seventy-five years old. They were uniform and each painted the same light blue color, which I found odd. Normally, houses varied a little bit. "Your homes are nice."

"Yes, my grandfather built them when we first settled in Athens." Barry beamed with pride. "He had a military background and knew that the best way to organize a neighborhood was to have the same houses. The lack of favoritism helps maintain control of the pack."

"Your house is a little different." His house was twice the size of the others. Granted, it was painted the same blue shade.

"Well, that's because it's the alpha's house." He patted himself on the chest. "Because of our extra work and responsibility, we deserve something more special." He looked over his shoulder at me. "Don't you agree?"

I wanted to say no, but that would cause more suspicion. Yes, being a leader laid responsibility on your shoulders, but it didn't mean I was special. To me, it meant the opposite. We had to worry more than the others. "Isn't that what America was founded on?"

"Smart woman." He led us toward a larger building with a concrete patio. "That's a dangerous thing."

The building was the size of two pack homes but had glass for the walls. Inside, a large television sat on one wall and an L-shaped black couch with a recliner on each side faced it. A table was set in the back with a checkerboard sitting on it. This had to be the pack's common area.

Wow, backhanded compliments. Aidan's shoulders tensed. *He's just like my dad.*

Really? Aidan never acted like that. Even when Jacob had carried my things to class, Aidan had sounded disgusted ... like he'd expected me to take care of myself, which was the opposite of how Barry acted.

"You only have stupid women in your pack?" Gabby asked from the very back.

I wanted to punch her. We weren't here to start a fight but rub elbows with Barry and find the girl. The girls knew she was here just like I did. We didn't need a mind link to figure that out.

"And you all are funny." Barry's dry laugh sounded forced.

We were playing a game of chess, one I hoped we could win.

At least ten women were setting the tables, grilling, and pulling out side dishes.

"This is the hard work our women contribute to our pack." Barry stepped onto the patio. "The rest of the pack will be here momentarily. I called for them just now."

Ten black-wired rectangle tables with eight black-wired seats at each table stood on the patio.

"How big is your pack?" It would be good to have numbers for future reference.

"We have sixty members here, but a few of our kids are

away at college." The alpha headed to the table closest to where the women were putting out fried potatoes, collard greens, deviled eggs, and a few other items. "But when everyone is here, we're around seventy."

A girl close to our age came out of the building, carrying mac and cheese. She walked to the end of the table they were setting the food on and placed the tray down.

My eyes immediately went to the area behind her left ear and discovered a birthmark. The top vertex of the star was in plain view for everyone to see.

That didn't make any sense. Why would they let her walk around like a normal pack member? They were part of The Hallowed Guild. How was this possible?

CHAPTER EIGHT

"Is everything okay?" Barry asked me as he walked over to the girl with the mark. "Looks like you've seen a ghost."

I fought against the natural urge to avert my eyes. That would make me look guilty. "Oh, no. Her tattoo caught my eye."

Aidan kept his gaze forward. *Smart move.*

That's becoming obvious. We had to outsmart him. *I only hope the others follow our lead.*

They were chosen for a reason just like you. Aidan's confidence was the boost I needed.

"There's a very interesting story to it." Barry touched the girl's shoulder, and she flinched. "It's the mark of the unfortunate.

"Really?" Gabby asked combatively. "How so?"

I turned around and gave her a warning look. If she let her anger get the best of her, we'd all be screwed.

"Oh, it's the mark of a curse." Barry touched the mark with his pointer finger. "Many packs aren't aware, but this could be the end of all shifters."

"Daddy." The girl's voice wavered as she turned toward us.

Wait ... that couldn't be possible, but as I took in her brown hair and eyes and her facial structure, it hit me hard. She was his child.

"Have you forgotten that you aren't allowed to call me that?" Barry asked hatefully.

"Of course, I'm sorry." She recoiled, preparing for physical punishment.

This guy was the ultimate asshole.

"You're forgiven, this one time." Barry dropped his hand. "But it's your only reprieve."

She nodded and cast her eyes down.

Endora hadn't been kidding when she'd said each drop of her blood had its own demons.

"Is it something she was born with, or did the affliction come later?" Aidan intertwined his fingers with mine.

Aidan asking these questions would make it seem like he wasn't a Murphy. "And how will she end us all?" I might as well help out.

"Good questions." Barry smirked with approval. "She's a hybrid half-witch, and her kind is determined to end us."

"If she's your daughter, that means you slept with a witch." Logan walked through our group and sat at the table closest to us. "Why would you do that if you hate witches so much?"

"Because I was young and let a witch seduce me." Barry hung his head in shame. "I'm so embarrassed to admit it, but that was before I became the pack's alpha and understood the magnitude of the curse."

"Curse?" He needed to believe we were clueless.

"Ahh, the one that will allow more packs to have

women alphas," he spat. "I know your pack doesn't have issues, but it's not how things were done in the past."

"If you are so against the idea, why didn't you kill your daughter?" Ivory's shoulders tensed.

She probably didn't want to hear the true answer.

"Because she's my blood." Barry mashed his lips together. "I couldn't kill my own child."

He almost appeared sincere.

Don't be fooled. Aidan squeezed my hand. *My dad is just like him. Charismatic. Don't forget how she flinched, expecting him to punish her. He is not a good guy.*

I'd almost forgotten that. *You're right.*

A few other male pack members joined us on the patio, and Barry introduced them. They were soon talking pack business, so our group of ten moved to a table. Beth grabbed a chair from another one and squeezed in between me and Ivory.

"This is bullshit." Gabby stood and swirled her finger around the group. "Let's go out back for a minute."

Logan's brows furrowed. "What for?"

"You'll see." Gabby turned on her heel and marched past the alpha and his pack members.

"She is one for theatrics." Ada sighed. "Let's go see what she wants."

Our group followed after her, and when we passed Barry, he grabbed Aidan's arm. "Is everything all right?"

"Oh, yeah." He motioned to where Gabby had walked to. "Gabby wants to talk to us about something. She's upset."

"Dinner will be ready soon, so don't take long." Barry huffed unhappily.

"We should only be a moment." Aidan hurried after the others.

We walked across a small grassy field to reach her.

"What the hell is going on?" Beth whispered so the others couldn't hear us.

"Us not being a pack is causing problems." Gabby blew out a breath and locked her eyes on me. "We should become a pack so we can communicate, and Emma should be our alpha."

"Are you serious?" I agreed that not linking had caused problems, but I hadn't expected her to volunteer me as alpha. Especially, since she was so against it during our drive to dinner.

"You found us and started this whole thing." Honor brushed her hand on my arm. "It makes sense for you to lead us. You're the one we can all agree on."

"A woman alpha?" Remus chuckled. "I never thought I'd see the day, but I'm good with that decision too."

"Wait ... you'll submit to me too?" I'd only expected the marked women to do that.

"Of course. I want to be part of the same pack as Ivory." He wrapped an arm around his mate. "And I'd be honored to be part of your pack."

"Then, let us begin." Sunny met my eyes and then lowered hers to the ground, submitting to me. A warm connection sprung in my chest.

The next three marked girls followed suit with Beth, Ada, Remus, Logan, and then Aidan submitting in succession.

You don't have to do that. Aidan was my mate, my equal, and Beth wasn't even part of this. She had her pack back home.

It's done. His warm words made me feel full of love.

And I've been with you since the beginning. Beth lifted an eyebrow. *There's no getting rid of me now.*

Their support in particular meant the most to me.

My link with the Rogers pack had now been replaced with a link to my own. *I'm honored you've chosen me.*

Don't make me regret it, Logan said tersely.

Now, that felt more like him. *We need to get back before they come looking for us.*

When we reached the patio, several more shifters had arrived.

"Is everything okay?" Barry squinted. "I'm assuming you had one of those emotional reactions women tend to have for no reason."

I linked with Gabby. *We told him you were upset.*

"People, in general, are a pain in the ass." Gabby swatted at the air. "Sometimes it gets overwhelming."

"Interesting. But you are a woman." He heaved a sigh, but his suspicion increased. "Oh, well. Why don't we sit and eat? The women will come by and serve us."

I want to scratch that smug look off his face. Gabby grumbled. *I bet this woman could kick his ass.*

She probably could. *Please, just try to stay calm.* The thought of food almost had my stomach rumbling again, so I focused on Barry's words. "I can make my own plate."

"No, I insist." Barry stepped in front of me, blocking my access to the table. "That's how it's done here. You wouldn't want to insult me."

If we don't listen, he'll cause a scene, and we could reveal who we are. Aidan touched my arm. *Let's go sit down.*

Against my better judgment, I listened. We couldn't start a war or battle here. We were severely outnumbered. Once we'd settled back in our seats, I closed my eyes to pull myself together.

The marked girl passed out plates to the men who sat

around chatting. The other women were still cooking and gathering everything.

I can't believe they're actually serving these assholes, Beth grumbled. *We should all be serving ourselves and eating together.*

This is what we're used to. Honor placed her hands in her lap.

And it's how every Hallowed Guild pack does it. Aidan grabbed the glass of water from the table. *It's not right, but we can't make a stink and make him even more wary.*

Times like these brought to attention how damn lucky I'd been to grow up in the Rogers pack. *It's so weird. That's not how I was raised.*

Me neither. Beth moved to the side as the marked girl placed her plate of food in front of her. *I'm not sure if we're normal or abnormal now.*

"Do you need any help?" It only seemed right to ask.

"No, I'm good." The girl jerked back. "Thanks for asking." She hurried to pick up a few more plates and headed back our way.

When she placed the plate down in front of me, I couldn't keep my mouth closed. "How long have you had the tattoo?"

"Since birth." She hid the pentagram point behind her hair.

Wait ... *I'd assumed he knew what she is because the witch gave birth to her, but she's had the mark since birth, like me.*

It makes sense since both of you are descended from the original witch. Aidan grabbed a fork and knife and cut a piece of his rare steak.

Think about it. Sunny popped a bite of mac and cheese into her mouth. *You had to prove you were worthy to begin the curse, and she has to prove she's worthy to end it.*

You mean prophecy ... Gabby growled.

Doesn't this feel like a curse to you? Sunny rubbed her neck where her mate had cut it. *It sure feels like it to me.*

I couldn't argue with that.

A text alert sounded, and Sunny pulled her phone from her pocket. She glanced at the screen and stiffened. *It's Eric.*

Even though the two of them had only seen each other for a few minutes, they each recognized the fated mates' pull. Eric was an alpha of The Hallowed Guild back in Austin, Texas. He had planned on killing Sunny because of her mark, but he couldn't do it. He had cut her throat so the pack would think he'd killed her, but then he'd carried her to safety. That was where we'd met them. They'd gotten closer over the past few weeks via phone calls and text messages. *Is everything okay?*

He wants to know if we're here. She placed her phone on the table. *Barry has alerted the other packs about us.*

Which is what I'd thought this entire time and why we needed to use our other names. Aidan chewed his food slowly.

We can't leave now or we'd confirm his suspicions. Remus surveyed the people around us. *Right now, they aren't paying a ton of attention to us.*

It's probably because our marks are covered and we pretended not to know anything about her mark. Honor moved her food around her plate with her fork. *We have to be careful.*

No more asking about her mark until we can get her alone. Aidan nibbled his bottom lip. *We have to be smarter than they are.*

They're typical, inflated ego alpha males that aren't

smart, so that shouldn't be hard. Beth winked at me. *We women can run circles around them.*

Damn straight we can. Gabby lifted her cup in salute.

THE REST of the evening passed without much action. Barry talked to us a little more, and we thanked him for the invitation.

He almost seemed disappointed that we were leaving, but I chalked that up to us not raising any more suspicion.

We tried hanging around as long as we could. I wanted to talk to his daughter alone.

Unfortunately, when it was time for us to leave, the girl had already gone.

We'd missed our opportunity.

Well, this night was a bust. Beth complained, using our new connection.

At least, we know where she is. That solved one piece of the puzzle. It also made it more problematic, especially since Barry didn't trust us.

As we walked out into the woods, the wind picked up and shifted directions, blowing into us. That's when I picked up her scent. *Wait, she's nearby.* I took off, following her scent.

I found her about five miles from the pack grounds, sitting next to a pond and staring at her reflection. Dark purple bruises marked her arm, and tears ran down her cheeks.

Give me a second and stay out of sight. If we all descended on her, we'd spook her.

I approached her slowly like I would a caged animal.

She tensed, but that was the only sign that she knew I was there.

"Hey." I kept my voice low and friendly.

Don't sound like a creepy psycho. Beth snorted in my mind.

Great, I'd totally missed the mark. "Are you okay?" I asked, using my normal low voice.

Better.

The girl wiped the tears from her face and turned around. Her eyes were still glassy, but she tried hiding the fact she'd been crying. "Oh, I'm fine." Her voice wavered on the edge of hysteria.

"It doesn't seem like you are." I slowed my pace even more but continued my trek toward her. "Did something happen?"

"What?" Her eyes widened, and she vehemently shook her head. "No."

"Then, what are those marks on your arm?" I didn't want to call her a liar, but I'd make it clear that I knew something.

"I accidentally spilled some water on a pack member." She rubbed the marks softly. "I deserved it for being so careless."

"Really?" They were abusing her emotionally and phys-ically. "I'm not so sure I agree."

"Look, that's how all packs work." Something akin to hope filled her eyes. "Don't they?"

"Nope." If she needed hope, I'd give it to her. "You could come with us." I wanted to say more, but I'd been warned to make her earn my trust.

"Oh, God no." She stood and stumbled back a step. "I must stay here as penance."

"For what?" She was too timid to have done something horrible. It sounded crazy.

"For being born." She cast her eyes to the ground and rubbed her mark. "I'm evil and should be killed. However, my dad is making me stay alive despite my pleas."

"How does a birthmark make you evil?" He'd totally fucked with her head.

"I'm part witch," she said with so much hate. "I'm cursed and marked for death." She held out her wrist, and there were so many damn cuts on it. "Every time I try to kill myself, he knows before I can go deep enough."

He knew through his bond with her.

"He won't let me die. He says I have to make up for what I am before he'll grant me that privilege." She scratched her nails into her skin. "He says it'll be soon, so my suffering is almost over."

"What is your name?" My heart broke watching her.

"It's Endora." She stilled and hurried back toward the pack. "I'm sorry. I've got to go."

I wanted to yell "Stop," but words were failing me. The jackass had gone so far as to give her the original witch's name and had her so screwed up that she wouldn't willingly come with us. We had only one option left, and we needed to devise a good plan to make it happen.

CHAPTER NINE

W*e have to grab her.* There was no way the alpha would allow us back here. He'd hoped to discover who we were and hold us hostage. We'd slipped under his radar, but the more we were around him, the riskier it would be. *This may be our only chance.*

Are you serious? Honor whipped her head toward me. *We're going to abduct her?*

You saw how she's brainwashed. Barry sucked so hard. Death would've been a better alternative than that kind of abuse. *What do you think?*

Aidan and Logan rushed after her, willing to do what I'd asked.

They can't do it alone. I pushed my legs to catch up to them.

Beth ran beside me. *You know this is illegal?*

Yes, but what other options do we have? It bothered me that this was our best alternative.

No, I think it's badass. Beth chuckled. *You're no longer the timid freshman I met in August.*

Badass probably isn't the right word. More like desperate.

What the fuck did you do? Aidan's panicked voice filled the bond.

Something wasn't right. We reached them in the next second and found Endora unconscious on the ground.

She was going to alert the pack if we didn't do something. Logan bent down and picked her up. *Now, we better run before they get worried about her.*

He was right. *Let's go!* I shouted in our pack bond, and we raced back toward the car.

The others caught up with us, and Sunny gasped, *Did he hurt her?*

He had to. Gabby kept up with her mate.

Let's focus on getting back to the Suburbans. The more we argued, the slower we'd be.

We flew through the woods faster than usual. If they figured out what we'd done and caught up with us, there would be no getting out of this alive.

Silence descended among the group as adrenaline coursed through us. The trees blurred past as we ran as fast as our legs could carry us. The howl of the pack would come at any second.

Right as the vehicles came into view, the alpha howl filled the air. I wasn't quite sure how we'd gotten that lucky, but I'd take it. *Get in the same vehicle you were in on the way here.*

I opened the back passenger door so Logan could get in easily. *Be careful not to hit her head again.*

As he brushed past me, I noticed a small trickle of blood running down her face.

At least, it wasn't a huge gash. With Logan, it could've been much worse.

Everyone got in the vehicles, and Aidan squealed out of the parking lot.

Luckily, the park was empty, and there were no rangers around. He burned rubber as he floored it on the main road, leaving a trail of smoke behind.

Oh, thanks, Beth grumbled through the bond. *Now I get to smell that all the way back to the hotel.*

We aren't staying there tonight. We would have to head straight back to the coven with Endora.

We need to grab our stuff, Logan interjected. *He obviously doesn't mind using witches, so we need to get our clothing so he can't locate us.*

I hadn't even considered that. *True, but let's make it a quick in and out.*

I'm assuming inappropriate laughter would be frowned upon? Beth giggled.

Aidan rolled his eyes. *Right now, yes.*

I removed the phone from my pocket and dialed Amethyst's number.

She picked up on the second ring. "Is everything all right?"

"No, not really." I filled her in on what had happened. "Since you guys are thirty minutes out, you'd better hurry and drop off the rental car. We'll meet you there."

"It'll be closed, so ..." She trailed off as Samuel piped in, "There's a key drop-off. It'll be fine."

"Great, we'll see you there." I hit END and placed my phone on the center console.

Aidan placed his hand on my arm. "Everything will be okay."

"You can't promise that." It was time to be realistic. *I wish things had gone differently.*

You mean that she'd come with us of her own free will?

Aidan scanned the road in front of us. *To be honest, we had a good streak going. We were bound to run into one person who would refuse to leave.*

But I didn't even ask her. That was the root of the problem. I'd taken away her choice.

You do realize we were all there, watching the conversation. Ivory leaned forward and placed her hand on my shoulder. *She wouldn't have come willingly. You made the right call.*

She'll need some deprogramming, though. Honor's sympathy flowed through our bond. *Hell, I wasn't abused as badly as she was, and I'm struggling.*

I had no clue. What a good leader I was turning out to be.

Why would you? Ada joined the conversation. *It's hard knowing what to do with someone breathing down your neck and threatening you.*

Gabby scoffed. *But you two never listened.*

Well, we tried bucking the system, but it never worked. Honor sounded ashamed. *So, with all of you guys, it's weird.*

If you ever need to talk, I'm here. I wanted them to know I would be there for them, no matter what.

We know, and that's what's kept us sane. Warmth filled the spot where Honor linked to me.

The Holiday Inn sign appeared ahead, and we made a plan. *Gabby, are you good getting your and Logan's stuff so he can stay here with her?*

Yeah. Gabby not being combative was a nice change of pace.

Logan, be prepared to drive off if needed. We had to cover all our bases.

On it. Logan shifted, ready to follow through.

I'll get in the other car so we can get away fast if shifters show up, Ivory said as the car stopped, and she jumped out, taking Beth's spot in the Suburban.

Sounds good. We were finally working as a team.

Everyone except Ivory and Logan were back in our rooms in minutes. Luckily, Aidan, Beth, and I hadn't unpacked since we'd been tied up with getting the witches settled. Aidan walked into our bedroom and stopped short.

I almost ran into his back but managed to plant my feet without falling over. *What's wrong?*

This. He moved aside, and the stench of foreign wolves slammed into my nose. Our clothes were strewn all over the floor, and all of the drawers were open.

Aren't we glad that the witches didn't stay with us? This had been my fear, and unfortunately, it'd been a valid one.

I shouldn't be surprised. Aidan entered the room and began picking the clothes up from the floor. *I expected this.*

Expecting it and seeing it are two different things. Beth breezed past me and began gathering her clothing.

Was everyone's room ransacked? I used our link to check in on the others. Hopefully, it was just ours.

Yes. Hostility laced Gabby's words. *Our clothes are everywhere.*

Ours too, Ada confirmed. *We're grabbing as much of our stuff as possible.*

Thankfully, Amethyst took the map, so there was nothing incriminating left behind. Well, other than kidnapping the alpha's daughter. *Let's hurry. They could be here any second.*

You don't have to tell us that, Gabby snapped.

Anger filled my body, and I wanted to go into their room and put her in her place, but our lives were more important.

We'll be ready in a couple minutes, Honor linked without being a smart ass.

Needing to help Aidan and Beth, I gathered items off the floor, sorting them between hers and ours. It only took minutes to get everything together.

Right as we'd finished, someone pounded on the hotel door. The scent of an unknown shifter floated through the cracks around the door.

They're here. I took in another deep breath. *There are two of them.*

Are they really going to attack us in a hotel full of humans? Beth zipped her bag on the bed. *That's crazy.*

That's why they're outside our room. Aidan scanned the room. *There's no way out but through that door.*

Knuckles pounded on the door again.

We'll have to answer. There was no getting around it. *Are you guys ready? We need assistance.*

What's going on? Remus asked.

We have two shifters. I stepped toward the door. "Just one minute." *Come help us when you hear the door open. If we don't get out of here quickly, it'll give the others time to show up.*

Our chance to escape was quickly dwindling.

Let me open the door. Aidan placed our bag on the bed and went straight to the door. He flipped the latch so the door would only open a smidgen. "Who is it?"

Someone kicked the door so hard it broke the latch and slammed against the wall.

"You have something of ours." A tall, greasy-haired man entered the room, followed by a younger, more well-groomed man.

"We do?" The less suspicious we acted, the better. "I'm not sure what you mean." I faced the room. "It's just the three of us here."

"You wouldn't by chance know where a certain female

pack member is?" The greasy-haired man perused the room, and his sights landed back on us.

None of us answered. He'd smell a lie if we did.

"Well, it's obvious that she's not in this room." Aidan lifted his chin, meeting the gross guy's eyes dead-on. "So ... that should give you our answer."

The younger guy stepped toward me and touched my arm. "It'd be sad to ruin that gorgeous face of yours."

I wanted to flinch away, but that was the exact reaction he desired. "You expect to walk in here and threaten us without proof?" The answer was obvious, but we had a game to play. The longer we did, the more time the enemy wolves had to get into position.

In a flash, the guy fisted my hair and yanked my head back. "You look even hotter like this." His arousal saturated the air.

"Get away from my mate," Aidan threatened.

"Or what?" The young guy smirked and lowered his nose to my neck.

That's all I needed. I rammed my knee into his crotch, and he sagged against me with a groan.

"What the hell?" the greaser asked and hurried over to me, but Aidan slammed him into the wall.

Aidan reared back and punched the guy in the face over and over again.

I dropped the younger man to the ground, letting him whither in agony on the dirty carpet.

Beth kicked the guy in the ribs several times. "Never touch my bestie like that."

He clutched his side with one hand and grabbed his balls with the other, like that would do him any favors.

Remus busted into the room right as Greaser pushed

Aidan off him. Remus ran over and grabbed Greaser's arms, tugging them behind his back.

We had to get out of here and fast. I raised my elbow and brought it down hard on the pervert's head, knocking him out.

"Damn." Beth glanced from me to the guy on the ground. "I didn't know you had it in you."

"Maybe you should follow her lead," Remus groaned as he struggled to keep the guy's hands locked in his grip.

"Noted." Aidan swung his fist right in Greaser's upper jaw, and he slumped against Remus.

"About time." Remus let go of the guy, and he hit the ground with a thud. "Let's go." He spun on his heel and headed out to where the other shifters waited in the hallway.

Aidan grabbed our bag and Beth's.

Aw, look at who's being all gentlemanly. Beth smacked my arm. *You're getting him trained.*

Maybe this whole pack link thing was a bad idea. Aidan shifted the bags' straps on his shoulder. *Now I have to deal with her smack talk mentally?*

You love it. Beth pointed at him. *Don't lie.*

I held back a smile since we didn't have time for this. *It's time.* I turned my back on them and headed out into the hallway.

All five of them were on high alert, surveying the area for threats.

We should take the elevators. If more shifters came here, they'd likely take the stairs, hoping to find us faster. They'd expect us to do the same thing when we left. *Humans could be there with us, protecting us.*

Okay. Sunny pressed the down button, which she'd been standing next to.

Logan connected with us. *How much longer are you guys going to be?*

We're on our way down now. We ran into a few snags. That was a simple way of putting it.

You've got ten more snags heading your way then, Logan said with alarm. *I saw them before they got to the car and dived in the middle row. The dark windows hid us back there.*

And they didn't look too hard in this one because I hid in the footwell. Ivory's voice shook a little. *They smelled you all and hauled ass to the hotel.*

I need to come help you, Logan said determinedly.

No, stay with her. If we left Endora alone, she could get away if she woke up. *We've got enough people here.*

The elevator door slid open, and cold fear crawled down my spine. When I saw it was empty, I almost cried with relief. *Let's go.*

This door would open in the lobby, so the shifters wouldn't attack us right away. The dark sky wouldn't do us any favors with their wolf vision, but at least we could get out the door. *Start the car.*

Already on it, Ivory responded.

So am I, Logan interjected as well.

The elevator dinged, and we stepped out into the lobby.

A shifter stepped into the stairwell, but he paused and looked in our direction. He changed course, heading directly toward us.

Let's go. Run as fast as you can. I don't care if humans are around. We had to get out of here. The longer it took, the more of a chance the wolves had to descend upon us. *Gabby, join us in our Suburban; everyone else, get into the other vehicle, and head straight to the coven. We'll pick up the witches and be only minutes behind you.*

Got it, Ivory replied. *The doors are unlocked, so hurry.*

The hotel staff watched in confusion as our group ran out the doors with our bags, only slowing for the automatic doors.

Once outside, Beth, Remus, and Sunny ran toward the second Suburban, and Logan opened the back door of the one Aidan had been driving.

Footsteps pounded behind us, alerting us that the reinforcements were catching up.

My hands became sweaty as I reached the passenger door. I wiped them off on my jeans, yanked the door open, and climbed in.

Everyone got in before Aidan threw our bag in the back, jumped behind the wheel, and gunned the engine. A shifter jumped in front of the car like he thought that would make us stay put.

Aidan pressed the gas, and the car lurched in the shifter's direction.

It turned into a game of chicken, and the shifter realized he would lose.

Right at the last moment, he jumped out of the way, narrowly avoiding the vehicle.

Another shifter tackled the side of the vehicle so hard we tipped onto two wheels before falling back on all four wheels.

An officer ran out of the hotel with a gun in his hands. He pointed it at the shifters as we pulled out onto the main road.

Now, we had to get the witches and get out of town.

CHAPTER TEN

"The cops won't be able to detain them for long." Aidan focused on the road ahead, driving way too fast. "If he's like my dad, he'll have an in at the sheriff's office."

"Getting a ticket wouldn't bode well, though." This was damn crazy. The secret society almost sounded like the mafia. "They'd have us pulled over and at their mercy."

"The rental place is right there." Aidan motioned to the building coming into view. "Once they get in, I'll slow down, but we'll be vulnerable until we get out of this city."

"You're right. They could pull us over for any reason." This scared me. How were six young girls supposed to win against a centuries-old society?

Our three friends stood next to the building and headed toward us as Aidan stopped.

Amethyst opened the back door and climbed in. "What happened?"

"We'll tell you on the way." Aidan scanned the area.

The three of them slid into the middle row, and we were back on the road in seconds.

Samuel turned toward the back and gaped at Endora. "Why is there a girl passed out in the backseat?"

"She wouldn't willingly come with us." Now that I'd spoken those words out loud, they sounded terrible.

"Wait ..." Coral leaned over the center console to see my face. "You kidnapped someone?"

"She did what had to be done," Logan said with respect. "She shocked me, but I'm glad she proved me wrong."

I linked to only Aidan. *If Logan approves, I'm not sure I made the right call.*

His shoulders shook with laughter. *I needed that.* He took my hand. *You made the right call. Don't doubt yourself. You've never had to make a decision like that. There have always been other options. Logan thrives off chaos, so he thought you were weak. He sees that you can make tough calls now. It's a good thing. Those two might fall in line.*

Why would anyone enjoy chaos? My life had been chaotic since I'd stepped foot onto Crawford University's campus. Between seeing Aidan again after he'd disappeared for over four years and forming my own my pack, my life was unrecognizable. Now that I was no longer part of the Roger's pack I had to call my parents before they freaked out.

Because those two counted on chaos to feel like they were part of something, Aidan said, answering the question I'd forgotten I'd asked. *They didn't have a stable home.*

That made sense and even softened me toward them some. I hadn't considered it. *I'm calling Mom.* I took my phone from my pocket and dialed her number.

It rang a few times before her comforting voice filled the line. "Hey, baby. How are you?"

"I'm okay." They already felt me pulling away, so this would be hard. "How are you doing?"

"Your father got an urgent call from Sam." Mom sounded tense. "He's heading straight here from town."

"I know why he called you." They should hear the news from me. "Look, something happened."

"What?" Her anxiety was palpable.

"It's nothing bad." Being an alpha was coveted, so they should be proud. "Mom, I ..." This shouldn't have been so hard. "I'm an alpha of my own pack."

Silence filled the line for a second.

"So, you're no longer part of our pack?" she asked indifferently.

"No, I'm sorry." Maybe I had it wrong. "It just kind of happened."

"How does starting your own pack just kind of happen?" A small sob escaped her.

"It's hard to explain." I hated keeping things from them. "I promise it wasn't premeditated. I wouldn't have gone through with it without talking to you first."

She sniffed. "So, you're never coming home?"

"No, I am." Wait ... that wasn't the truth. "I mean, I'll come visit." My home wasn't there anymore.

"But you won't stay to start a family?"

"No." I couldn't lie, not to her. "Jacob made it clear that Aidan wouldn't be welcomed anyway. My home is with him, and you know two alphas can't live together." Sam and I would be at each other's throats.

"I feel like I'm losing you," she whispered.

"No, you aren't." They'd been there for me and taken me in as part of their family. "Think of it as us growing. You'll visit us all the damn time. Just give me more time to finish this."

"Okay." She cleared her throat. "I love you."

"I love you too." I wished I could be there for her and

comfort her more. I had to end this soon so we could move on with our lives. I ended the call and stared out the window.

Everything will be okay, Aidan said, trying to comfort me.

We were on the main interstate, leaving Athens behind us and heading back to the coven. I'd hoped to feel more relaxed the farther we drove, but it was the opposite. The girl would wake soon, and Barry could track her with the pack link. We had to figure something out fast. "Is there a way to block pack magic?"

Amethyst shifted, squirming away from Samuel, who sat in the middle. "What do you mean?"

"Ugh," Gabby groaned. "The alpha bond. He can find her if we don't do something."

"That's why you don't take someone against their will." Coral sighed. "What the hell were you thinking?"

"You didn't see her," Aidan said, coming to my defense. "Her dad has her brainwashed. She wants to die because she's part-witch."

"Well, that's sunshine and rainbows." Samuel turned toward the backseat and glanced at her. "Holy shit, is she bleeding?"

"We had to knock her out." Logan sneered. "It's just a little blood, and she's already healed. It could've been much worse."

"He's right." The witches still hadn't warmed to Logan and Gabby, and I couldn't blame them. "And it was a good thing you guys didn't stay at the hotel. Our room was ransacked."

"Why the hell did you go back to the hotel room?" Coral gaped. "That was stupid."

"The alpha obviously didn't mind screwing a witch."

Gabby wrinkled her nose. "He wanted to have a hybrid to sink his claws into and brain fuck them. If he'd go that far, he also wouldn't mind using a witch to locate us."

"That's so sad." Amethyst frowned and shook her head. "Let me call Mom and see what she can find. I'm sure there's something we can do."

"It needs to be strong enough to hold until we can deprogram her." I had no clue how long that would take, and we were already running out of time.

A LITTLE AFTER ELEVEN, we pulled into the coven. Thankfully, it wasn't too far away from Athens, but we still had a lot of work to do before bed.

The others had arrived only a few minutes before us. They were at the back of the vehicle, pulling out the luggage, with Beatrice, Sage, and Rowan standing around.

Our group, except for Logan and Endora, got out of the car.

"Did you find a spell that would work?" Amethyst asked.

"Yes, we think we did." Beatrice pulled her daughter into a hug. "Where's the girl?"

"In the back with Logan," Gabby said and moved the seat forward so Logan had more room to climb out. "She's been out for several hours."

"Someone needs to perform a perimeter spell in case this doesn't work." Beatrice looked at Rowan. "Can you and Coral handle that while we get the girl set up in the house?"

"On it," Rowan agreed and grabbed Coral's arm. "Let's get Finn to help too. It'll go faster."

Aidan held his hands out toward the backseat. "Here, give her to me."

The girl's head was jostled from side to side as Logan placed her in Aidan's arms.

Samuel cringed. "She looks pretty out of it. I bet she'll feel it in the morning."

"If her neck doesn't snap first." Beth held Endora's head in place. "I mean, she looks like a bobblehead."

Ada chuckled and covered her mouth with her hands. "I'm so sorry. That was inappropriate."

Honor slapped her friend on the arm. "Behave."

"If that's the worst thing she experiences, it will be a blessing." Amethyst turned to her mother. "Is there anything we need to get for the spell?"

"Just her blood." Beatrice didn't appear happy. "It links her to her pack magic."

Sage said, echoing her son's sentiments, "Against her will?"

"It's not ideal." Beatrice headed toward the house. "But it's our only option unless you'd like to lead The Hallowed Guild wolf packs here. I'm sure the entire pack will come looking for her."

"Point taken." Sage nodded. "Let's get her in before she wakes up."

Logan jumped to the ground from the backseat, and he and Remus grabbed our bags before following us.

"For her to appear so small, she's stout." Aidan laid the girl on the couch.

Logan placed the bags by the door. "And I had to run with her to the Suburban, so I don't want to hear it."

"In all fairness, you didn't ask for help." Remus dumped the luggage and made his way next to Ivory.

"Well, it's a weakness." Logan stood straight and avoided our gazes. "Just forget I said anything."

Maybe she's not the only one who needs deprogramming. I huffed into Aidan's head.

It's part of the alpha males' nature to feel that asking for help makes us appear weak. Aidan brushed his hand along my arm. *So, give him a little slack.*

Valid point. "What do we need to do?"

"There's a small black bowl next to a dagger sitting on the kitchen table." Beatrice grabbed a pillow and placed it under Endora's head.

I found the items and brought them back to her.

"Mom, are you sure about this?" Amethyst tapped her foot. "I mean, she should have a choice."

"Her choice would be not to do it." Sunny patted her shoulder. "Believe me. We're protecting her. I promise."

Endora groaned and moved her head to the side.

"Shit, she's coming to." What we were doing made me sick to my stomach. "Is there anything else you need?"

"The spell book." Sage rushed to the coffee table and picked it up. "Okay, here it is."

Endora blinked and grabbed her head. "Oh God, where am I?"

With shaky hands, Beatrice picked up the dagger and brought the sharp edge to Endora's hand. "This might hurt."

Those had been the wrong words to say.

"What?" Endora sat straight up, and her bottom lip trembled. "Help!" she yelled.

Unfortunately, she wouldn't find the help she wanted here.

She yanked her hand from Beatrice's and swung her feet onto the floor, about to stand.

Here we went again. She had to be talking to her father.

Grab her now. I stole the dagger from Beatrice, ready to do the job on her behalf.

Aidan ran behind the couch and captured one arm, holding her in place, while Logan held the arm closest to me still.

"We don't have time to waste." I firmly gripped a finger and pricked it with the dagger.

"Ouch," she whined, thrashing against their grasps.

"I'm sorry, but we're doing what we think is best." The words cut like glass. I turned her hand over, and Beatrice held the bowl underneath as I squeezed out drops of her blood.

"You can't do this!" she cried as she shook with either rage or fear.

"Start the spell." I got that the witches were struggling with this task—hell, we all were—but this was life or death. "She's contacting them right now."

Sage muttered words that made no sense to me. The surrounding air began to charge, and Endora's eyes widened. She must have felt it.

"No, please, no." Her skin rippled, proving her wolf surged inside. "I've got to go back to him."

"Who is she talking about?" Samuel watched, wide-eyed, as the scene unfolded.

"Her father." I'd bet money on it.

Lightning struck outside the house.

Honor's head jerked toward the window. "What was that?"

"That's what happens when you take someone's blood against their will." Amethyst stood and paced the room. "The magic in the air causes so much friction that lightning takes hold."

Beth plastered herself against the wall. "Then, how the hell does black magic exist?"

"Haven't you noticed tragedy strikes when it's done?" Amethyst wrapped her arms around herself.

"Not exactly," Beth replied.

Lightning flashed through the window, hitting the floor inches from Gabby.

She jumped in the air and fell to her knees.

"Somebody save me." Endora gagged as friction chafed my skin.

The magic felt different from all of those times before. Now, I understood why they hadn't been thrilled about performing it.

The windows shook and vibrated in the howling wind. The lights flickered, and Sage's words became harder to hear.

"Is there something we can do?" I wanted to help fix this somehow.

"Finish the spell." Beatrice placed her hands on the girl and lowered her head.

The ground shook. Aidan crawled over to me and pulled me into his arms. *Stay here with me.*

We have to do something. Coral, Rowan, and Finn were setting up a perimeter spell. Were they okay out there?

"No!" Endora cried out before her body stilled and her head hit the pillow.

"It's done." Sage sighed with relief, and the wind calmed down.

The ground rattled as it settled underneath us, and the wind gently stirred outside.

The room remained silent; only our collective breathing could be heard.

"Is she okay?" Amethyst pressed her hand to Endora's forehead.

"Yes, it's just that I blocked all of her connections." Sage shut the book. "It overwhelmed her."

"How long will this spell last?" Ivory asked as Remus rubbed his hands along her shoulders.

"I ... I don't know." Beatrice sighed. "We'll need to do it every few days to make sure it holds."

We would have to go through all of this again? But right then, that wasn't my concern. I stood and rushed to the door, racing to check on Coral, Rowan, and Finn.

CHAPTER ELEVEN

Once outside the house, I sniffed the air and scanned the area. I didn't know what I'd expected, but this wasn't it. The moon shone brightly in the dark but cloudless sky. Besides the crack in the window, there was no indication that a storm had raged minutes before.

Aidan inhaled sharply and motioned toward the road. "They're this way."

The front door opened, and Amethyst rushed outside. "What's wrong?"

"We need to check on Finn, Coral, and Rowan." If the storm had attacked them as well, they might be in a horrible situation.

"They're fine." Amethyst gestured to the house. "Nature only attacked us because of the spell. It touched no one else."

"Are you sure?" I hated the thought someone might need us.

"Yes. We would've secured the neighborhood if the spell presented a threat," Amethyst said reassuringly. "And they should be back momentarily."

"Okay." I lifted my head toward the sky and collected myself. "That petrified me."

"Couldn't you have at least hinted that something like that could happen?" Aidan placed his hands on my shoulders and rubbed the knots.

I hadn't realized how tense I was.

"She was waking, and we all reacted." Amethyst opened the door. "I'm sorry we didn't think to warn you."

We followed her back in, and the shifters were still gathered next to the wall, in shock.

Beth's pale face had sweat along her forehead. "Well, that was a doozy." She placed a hand on her stomach. "I think I might puke."

"Go to the bathroom, then." Gabby took a large step away from her. "I don't want throw-up on my shoes."

"You're both so dramatic," Ada complained and headed into the kitchen. "Stress makes me hungry."

"Feel free to eat whatever you want." Beatrice didn't take her attention off Endora.

"How do you think she'll handle it?" I hadn't considered the ramifications for her.

"I'm not sure." Sage scratched her head. "Only time will tell. We've never performed a spell like this before."

"She won't be, like, a rogue wolf, will she?" Sunny asked with concern.

"Maybe." Sage shrugged. "We'll have to wait and see."

"I will say, she's out for the night." Beatrice stood and grabbed the green throw from the backrest of the couch and covered Endora.

That's when Coral, Rowan, and Finn entered the house.

"How'd it go?" Seeing them eased some of my anxiety.

See, Amethyst was right. They're okay. Aidan intertwined his fingers with mine.

"Fine." Coral yawned. "But it took a lot out of us. Granted, I'd rather be doing that than going through what you all did."

"Oh, you guys saw that?" Honor sounded surprised.

"We aren't blind." Rowan smirked. "But we weren't the ones nature was pissed at. I had to get an attitude with Finn, though, because he was determined to try to help you all from the onslaught like he could do something about it."

"Either that or toss a wolf or two out as a sacrifice." Logan sneered at him.

Finn's breathing increased. "That's not fair."

"It kind of is." I wished Logan had kept his mouth shut, but he wasn't wrong. Finn had been combative since the day I'd met him. "You haven't been the most welcoming."

"While you were gone, I thought about what you said, and you're right." Finn cast his eyes down. "If the original witch found you all worthy, I should too."

Beth walked around the room, looking down the hallway and in the pantry. "Where's the recorder?"

"What are you talking about?" Aidan's brows furrowed. "Why would there be a recorder?"

"Because he sounds sane for once, so it has to be a joke or a trap." She kept searching the house. "None of this makes sense."

Finn huffed and looked very uncomfortable.

"Okay, I think it's time we blow up the air mattresses and get some sleep." If he was trying, then her doubt would only hinder his efforts. "We're all tired and a little out of it."

"We were almost electrocuted." Remus finally budged from his spot. "That took the little bit of energy I had left."

"Let's get moving." Ivory headed toward the closet and pulled out the air mattresses.

"You two go ahead and take off." Beatrice nodded toward Aidan's and my bedroom. "I'll help them get set up."

I should have argued, but I was dead on my feet. "Are you sure?"

"Yes, go on."

Aidan and I didn't need any more encouragement to head to bed. Once I shut the door behind us, I almost collapsed. "Let me take a quick shower before bed." I needed to decompress or I'd toss and turn despite exhaustion.

A grin spread across his face. "Okay, go get in. I'll bring you a change of clothes."

"I love it when you talk dirty to me," I teased and made my way into the bathroom. I turned on the water and undressed while the shower heated.

Not soon enough, I stepped in. The warm water hit between my shoulder blades, releasing some of the tension.

The bathroom door opened, and Aidan stepped inside. "You doing okay in there?"

"Yeah." I raised my head to soak my hair.

"Your pajamas are on the sink."

"Thank you." Instead of hearing the door shut behind him, I heard the unzipping of his jeans and them falling to the ground.

The curtain moved, revealing my delicious mate in all his glory.

"What are you doing?" Despite trying to play it cool, my arousal scented the air.

"Thought you might need someone to wash your back." He joined me in the shower and moved forward, placing my back against the cool, white plastic wall as his lips claimed mine.

His minty taste filled my senses, and his hardness pressed against my lower stomach. A moan escaped as my hands slipped between our bodies, touching him. I stroked him, and a guttural groan vibrated in his chest.

That feels so good. His hand slipped between my legs, and his fingers circled on the spot only he knew about.

Damn. Every time with him felt better than the last, and I was already getting dizzy.

He increased the pressure, making me almost lose my mind.

God, you're beautiful, he whispered in my mind.

I pulled his hand away from my body. *I need you, please.* All sense of fatigue was gone, and I wanted him more than anything in the world.

Well, I can't say no to that. He grabbed my ass, hoisted me up, and slammed inside me.

I tightened my legs around his waist and wrapped my arms around his shoulders. He thrust into me over and over again, his lips never leaving mine.

The pleasure built, and I threw my head back, savoring the feeling of the water sliding down my face. He lowered his head, capturing my nipple and gently biting down.

My body bucked as the pleasure increased and pulsated throughout me. I rocked against him, riding it out.

He released my breast and grunted as he finished right after me.

We stayed in that position for a few more seconds before I stood.

That was incredible. He peppered kisses along my face and pressed his lips to mine.

Eh, it was okay. I couldn't inflate his ego too much.

Liar. He sucked my bottom lip.

My body warmed again. *Maybe.*

As much as I'd love round two, you need to rest. He squirted shampoo into his hand. *Now, turn around.*

What are you doing?

What do you think? He rubbed his hands together, making the shampoo sudsy. *Washing your hair. Now, turn around before I make you.*

Maybe I want to be made, I teased as I turned around so he could work on my hair.

His strong fingers massaged my scalp, and my body sagged against his. They were like magic, releasing all of the pent-up stress from my muscles.

Let's get you good and relaxed and get some rest. He kissed my neck and proceeded to take care of me.

AFTER TWO HOURS OF SLEEP, I found myself wide awake. An uncomfortable feeling pulsed through me, but I couldn't put a finger on the cause.

Aidan snored beside me, sleeping deeper than he had in weeks. Our shower had been fun, and we'd had the bonding time we'd needed for a while. As soon as we'd mated, our life had been in turmoil, and we hadn't been able to nurture our bond or spend time together like a newly mated couple should.

Not wanting to bother him, I slipped out of the bed, making sure I made no noise as I tiptoed to the door and opened it. Once the opening was wide enough, I paused before stepping through.

Loud snores, which the door had muffled, bounced off the walls. Between Beth and Logan, every single one of them had to be wearing earplugs. I scanned the room, and my eyes landed on an empty couch.

No.

My first instinct was to wake everyone up, but I'd hate for us all to descend on her again. Her scent was still strong, so she'd only left minutes ago.

Following her scent, I headed into the kitchen. The back door was ajar.

Smart girl.

Outside, I followed her trail into the woods. The nocturnal animals were crawling around, and an owl hooted in the distance. The cool nip in the air reminded me that fall was in full force.

The trees were thick, but I was gaining on her. I could hear her panicked breathing, so she was only a mile or so ahead.

Suddenly, her loud cry pierced the air.

Fear choked me as I raced toward her. "Endora!" I yelled, not worried about being heard.

When she came into view, she was placing her hands in the air, reminding me of a mime. She pounded against an invisible barrier, and a loud knocking sound returned. "Let me out!" she shouted.

"It's the perimeter spell." Thank God they'd put one up.

She spun around, her chest heaving. "I just want to go home."

"Why?" Her desperation to leave made no sense.

"Because Father needs me." She stepped back until she was against the barrier. "You don't understand. I'm not done serving him."

"Serving him? What does that mean?" Oh, please, God. Tell me he wasn't a complete sicko.

"If I don't receive his blessing, I can never die." She pulled at her hair like a damn crazy person. It hurt to watch. "I shouldn't be allowed to live."

"Why would you say that?" How the hell were we supposed to end the secret society when we had a nut job as part of our party?

"I'm part-witch." She wrinkled her nose and banged the back of her head against the barrier. "Not worthy of air."

I wanted to let her know I was part-witch too, but it didn't feel like the smart move. "You have every right to live." I took a few steps in her direction.

When her eyes opened wider, filling with even more fear, I stopped, not wanting to push her.

"No, I don't." She turned and ran toward the road that led into the neighborhood. "I have to leave."

I ran after her, but not so close that I'd appear too threatening. "Endora, please calm down."

"The longer I'm away from him, the angrier he'll be." She turned right and ran into the barrier. She clutched her arm to her side and took off again. "There has to be a break somewhere."

"It surrounds the entire coven." I needed her to see reason. She was so determined to get out that she wasn't acting rationally. "There is no way out unless they allow it."

"Then, I'll make them." She raced back toward our house. "That's the only way."

Well, I hadn't thought that one all the way through. Dammit, I would have to bother Aidan. *I need help.*

Huh? He sounded sleepy. After a few seconds, his voice was clear. *Emma, where are you?'*

I'm out here chasing Endora.

Alone? he growled.

He already knew the answer, so I wouldn't humor him.

We went out the back door, and the perimeter spell kept her from escaping. She's heading back to make a witch let her out.

I'll wake the others.

No, let's handle it ourselves. If we keep teaming up on her, she won't trust any of us. There had to be a way to get through to her.

Fine. Displeasure rolled through our bond. *Should I go out the back?*

Yeah, and run to the front. The houses were in view. *We should be there in a few minutes.*

Our link went silent, and now that we were close to the house, I increased my pace to catch up with her.

She glanced over her shoulder and almost stumbled. "Please, just leave me alone."

"You know we can't do that." I didn't want to lie to her like Barry had her entire life. "We're here to help you."

Aidan appeared in front of her, and she slowed to a stop.

"If you think you can force a witch to let you out with a pack of wolves and a coven there to protect them, you need to reconsider." I could try manipulating her like Barry had, but that would only make the situation worse.

"Why do you want me?" Tears streamed down her cheeks, leaving a trail of moisture behind. "I'm nobody."

"That's not true." The very thing she hated was what made her strong. "You're worth more than you know."

"He warned me about witches." Her eyes turned a grayish blue as her wolf surged forward. "He said that one day, a coven would try to take me, and there would only be one thing left for me to do."

Something's not right. Aidan approached her.

She was glaring at me and didn't even notice.

"If you could just listen ..." I wanted to shake some sense into her.

"No!" she screamed and raced toward me, hatred clear on her face. She lurched right at me, aiming to kill.

The last thing I wanted to do was hurt her, but if I didn't, she might kill me.

CHAPTER TWELVE

My wolf instincts surged forward, and I dodged her attempt to grab my neck. The bitch meant to either choke me or break it.

"Endora, come on." Keeping in mind the fact that we had kidnapped her, I understood she wasn't being irrational, at least, not with this.

"Let me go!" she screamed, her face turning tomato red.

"I would if we could." That wouldn't go over well.

I'm about to end this. Aidan was as still as a statue. *I understand you want to get through to her, but it won't work.*

She charged me again, and brown fur sprouted across her arm. Her wolf was almost in complete control.

"Please, Endora." I hated to admit it, but Aidan was right. She was scared out of her mind.

She countered my right pivot and rammed her fist right into the stomach. "I should've never told you my name."

I fell to the ground hard with her on top of me. She pulled her arm back, ready to punch me, when Aidan grabbed her hand.

Her body jerked at the sudden loss of momentum.

He yanked her off me and put her in a chokehold.

She bucked and screamed, but she couldn't break his hold.

Lights turned on in Beatrice's and Rowan's houses as the wolves woke up from the noise.

The front doors opened, and the shifters all rushed outside.

"What the hell is going on?" Breathing raggedly, Honor took in the scene before her.

"Endora tried to escape." My back throbbed from the way I'd landed, and I slowly stood.

"And tried to kill Emma twice," Aidan said almost inaudibly.

"Let me guess." Beth swatted at the air. "The dumbass let her."

Aidan's nostrils flared. "You better watch what you call her."

"Everyone calm down." Things were getting out of hand. "We captured the poor girl." Even though we'd done what we'd had to, it didn't make it right. That's what I'd learn so far. There really weren't any black and white areas. It was all gray, and you did the best you could with the information you had at your disposal.

"I want to go home." Endora lost some of her gusto. "Please."

"That won't happen." Gabby marched over and put her finger in Endora's face. "Whether you like it or not, we're your new family, so suck it up."

"But ..." Endora's bottom lip trembled.

"Cut the act." Gabby slapped her hard in the face. "You may be broken, but you aren't weak."

Something I didn't understand crossed Endora's face. "I don't know what you mean."

"Logan and I will handle it from here." Gabby fisted the girl's hair and dragged her back to Beatrice's house with Logan beside her.

I couldn't believe what I'd just seen. "We've got to do something."

"No, we don't." Honor paused and chewed on her lip. "She's kind of playing you."

"What? No." She seemed so sincere. "There's no way."

Ada lifted her hands. "We aren't saying she's not messed up. But she had to be smart to survive in a pack like that. All of them would have wanted her dead, not just her father."

"So, what are you saying?" I needed them to be blunt.

Ivory rocked on the balls of her feet. "She learned how to survive, and she might be weak with her father, but not us. She'll kill you the first opportunity she has."

Aidan bared his teeth. "She already tried twice."

"I'm an idiot." What they said made sense, so why hadn't I seen it right away?

"No, you're kind and think the best of everyone." Beth touched my arm. "You'll break through to her when we can't."

I wasn't so sure about that. "We need to keep an eye on her." Going after her alone had been a bad call. If I couldn't see what she was capable of, I'd need to keep someone around who could.

"Is everything okay?" Beatrice's brow creased, and she walked toward us in fuzzy, brown house shoes.

"Endora tried to escape, but the perimeter held her in." I hated to think what would've happened if it hadn't. She might be blocked from the pack bond, but she could easily call her dad from somewhere.

Beatrice rubbed her hands along her bare arms, fighting

off the night's chill. "I'm not surprised. That's why I had three witches spell it."

"You can't blame her for trying." Remus tucked his hands under his armpits with his thumbs visible and pointing upward. "And that's a good sign for us. That means she's a fighter."

"As long as we convince her to side with us." There had to be a way to connect with her.

"What everyone needs is a good night's rest." Beatrice gestured to the house. "Beth, you're welcome to join us if you'd like."

"Oh, hell no." Beth cringed. "I like having a real bed to sleep in."

"It must be nice." Ada snickered as she headed toward the house. "I get to sleep on the ground."

"Your choice." Beth patted her shoulder.

"Nope, we all agreed we'd sleep together in the family room like a pack with the couples rotating out the spare bedroom. Besides, I like listening to the sounds of Emma and Aidan getting it on." Ada spread her arms apart. "At least, someone is getting some."

Save me now. "You cannot." We didn't have sex as much as either of us would like. "We were in the shower earlier."

"Really?" Beth's mouth dropped. "Are you sharing or bragging?"

Sunny's laughter added fuel to the fire.

"What? No." I couldn't believe how drastic of a turn this conversation had taken. *Kill me, please.* "You said you heard, so I ..." I trailed off. There was no salvaging this.

Aidan wore a huge smile on his face. *Nope, I'm enjoying this too much to interfere.*

You know, it's kind of nice. I almost felt like a teenager. *I can't remember the last time we goofed around like this.*

I'd agree if you hadn't been attacked. Aidan took my hand and pulled me against his side. "All right, I'm taking my mate back to bed."

"I bet you are," Remus scoffed.

It was time to go.

"What's wrong, Emma?" Beth cooed as her shoulders shook with laughter. "Your face is beet red."

Not dignifying that with a response, I marched into the house and heard a loud conversation coming from the very back of the house, by our room

"Don't touch me," Endora rasped.

"We need to make sure you don't run away again," Logan's impatient voice boomed.

Oh, dear God. I rushed down the hallway as the others came back in from outside, and I took the first door on the right.

"Maybe we can work with her a little more," Amethyst said comfortingly. "There's no reason to go overboard."

I entered the room and came to a grinding halt. They had her hands and feet handcuffed to the maple headboard on the king-sized bed. "What in the world?" I was speechless.

Aidan stood next to me, taking in the scene. "It's not a horrible idea."

"See." Gabby pointed at Aidan. "Even he agrees."

"Where did you even get these?" I couldn't look away from the handcuffs.

"I always carry around a few." Logan shrugged. "It comes in handy at times."

I wasn't touching that with a ten-foot pole. I opened the

pack link, including everyone. *And how is chaining her up going to win her over?*

Logan's jawline hardened. *We have to contain her. It's harder for her to shift this way, and she can't sneak out and call someone. This isn't an ideal situation, so the solution won't be great either.*

I wanted to argue, but dammit, he had a point.

Honor interjected. *Why don't Ada and I sleep in the same room as her? With two of us there, she won't be able to take us out at the same time, and worst case, we holler for help.*

That's a good idea. Ada stood on my other side and took in the room. *There's plenty of room for us to cram in here. We can bring the air mattress in and move the bed to the side.*

The rooms here were decent-sized. It would be a tight fit, but it could work. *We can move the bed against the far left wall. It'll be away from the door and window.* She'd have to pass by two shifters to get to either exit.

Fine, let's be easy on her. Gabby rolled her eyes, informing us of how she really felt.

It's not about being easy on her. Aidan placed a hand on my arm for support. *It's about not ruining our relationship with her. We have to give her a reason to trust us.*

Let her go, I commanded. *We can't do this. It's not right.*

"I'll go get the air mattress." Logan tossed the keys to the handcuffs to Gabby. "I can't take much more of this." He pushed past Aidan, heading to the living room.

"Do we have to?" Gabby's shoulders deflated as she twirled the keys around her finger.

"Yes, we do." I couldn't argue too much; the girl had tried to kill me.

Gabby slowly made her way back to the bed.

"What's going on?" Fear filled Endora's face, and her bottom lip trembled. She jerked, but her handcuffs restrained her.

"I'm letting you out," Gabby complained. "They want me to."

Endora's brows furrowed. "Really?"

"Don't worry." If she thought she could try to kill me again, she was about to get a surprise. "Honor and Ada are going to sleep in the room with you."

Gabby unlocked the handcuffs, and Endora rubbed her wrists and ankles where she'd been restrained.

"Where will they sleep?" Endora asked.

"Logan is getting their air mattress." Aidan headed over to the bed and grabbed an edge.

She crawled to the other side. "What are you doing?"

"I wouldn't get that close to the end," I warned as he pushed the bed against the wall. "We have to make room for their bed."

Endora shivered. "I don't want to share a room. Can't I have this one to myself?"

"Not after you tried to kill Emma." Amethyst's hard tone caught me off guard. "Privileges are stripped when you try to hurt one of your own."

"I'm not one of you," Endora spat, spattering Aidan's face with spittle.

"Well, that was lovely." Aidan wiped the spittle away and stepped back. "I think I need a shower."

"If we'd kept her handcuffed, you wouldn't have that problem," Gabby muttered loud enough for everyone to hear.

Ada backed against the wall. "Just let it go."

"It's easy for you to say." Gabby narrowed her eyes. "You don't know anything about the outside world."

"What the fuck do you mean?" Honor flexed her fingers and popped her neck.

"You guys lived in the sticks." Gabby placed her hands on her hips. "And didn't get out much."

"Okay, that's enough." It was time for me to take control of the situation before it got worse. "It's late, and everyone's emotions are short."

"She's right." Amethyst rubbed her forehead like she had a headache. "We're all tired and overwhelmed."

Footsteps in the hallway alerted us to Logan right before he reentered the room. He had the mattress under an arm while Ivory trailed after him, carrying the pillows and covers.

He tossed the bed on the ground and scanned the room. "I guess the room is as secure as possible." He covered his mouth as he yawned. "Let's go back to bed."

"That's what we were just talking about." Gabby looped her arm through his, and as the two passed me, I snatched the keys from Gabby's hands. "I'll keep these for now."

"Fine. I guess it's back to an air mattress in the den" They continued to the room.

"I'm sorry about those two." Maybe Endora deserved how Logan and Gabby were treating her, but Logan was scary as hell with his silver hair, almost white eyes, and scar. His presence alone made people nervous, never mind if he was chaining you to a bed.

"Why are you being nice to me?" Endora stared at me like she was trying to solve a puzzle. "I tried to kill you."

"Because you didn't know any better." I didn't feel like pouring my heart and soul out to her. Exhaustion had finally hit me. "Do you need anything? If not, I'm going to get some rest too."

"No." The word sounded more like a question.

"Okay, let's go." Aidan intertwined his fingers with mine, and we walked out of the room together.

Honor followed behind us. "I'll push the mattress in front of the window and door when everyone gets out." She brushed her hand along my arm. "We'll link with you if we need anything."

Amethyst followed us out. "Goodnight, you two."

"Night." We walked down the hallway and headed straight back to our bedroom. My legs grew heavy with each step.

Aidan lay on the bed and opened his arms to me. *Are you okay?*

I'm fine. I cuddled against him, enjoying the warmth of his embrace. *I'm so tired. I've been struggling to sleep.*

Well then, let's try again.

I laid my head on his chest and let my eyelids shut.

A LOUD KNOCK sounded on the door, stirring me from my rest. It took a second for my brain to catch up with my ears.

It's Endora. Aidan's arm tightened around my waist. *We can tell her to come back later.*

We can't do that. Especially since it was her. We needed to make her feel important and valued. "Is everything okay?"

"No." Endora's voice cracked. "It's not."

I jumped to my feet and opened the door. "What's wrong?"

"It's a good thing I have pants on," Aidan grumbled as he grabbed his shirt from the side of the bed and slipped it on.

Endora blinked and cleared her throat. "Your cousin might need your assistance."

"Cousin?" It took a few seconds before it clicked. "Finn?"

"Yes. Someone informed him of what I tried to do last night, and he came stomping into my room." Endora straightened her shoulders. "And I did what I had to do."

"Which was?" I couldn't tell if she was upset.

Oh, come see for yourself. Ada laughed loudly in my head. *You won't want to miss out.*

"He came into the room, threatening me for hurting his cousin, and ignoring Beatrice when she asked him to stop." Endora scratched her nose. "So I handled it, but Beatrice asked me to get you to free him."

My stomach dropped. "Free?"

I raced into the room and saw something that I couldn't unsee.

CHAPTER THIRTEEN

Finn was handcuffed to the bed similar to the way Endora had been last night, but with "weak asshole" Sharpied on his forehead.

His nostrils flared. He mumbled some words, his focus on Endora, and suddenly, her brown hair turned fuchsia.

"Oh, my God." Ada snorted.

"What?" Endora surveyed the area.

"Your hair." Honor at least tried to restrain herself. "It's pink."

Endora picked up her hair, and her mouth dropped open. "Change it back."

"Let me out." Finn yanked against the cuffs like he expected them to fall off.

"I brought her here to do that." Endora marched over to him. "Change it back or she won't let you out."

"I'm confused." This had to be a crazy-ass dream.

"You aren't the only one." Aidan's brows furrowed. "How did this happen?"

"He charged into the room, ranting about her trying to kill you." Honor stood from the bed. "I guess he forgot about us being shifters because Endora knocked him out and handcuffed him. After writing her loving note, she headed to your room."

"Stop." Finn was an odd one. He hated shifters and tried to dislike me. But we were cousins, which made him feel conflicted. Even though he had betrayed us by talking to The Hallowed Guild, he'd made it clear that I was to be protected. "Once I let you loose, change her hair back."

"Fine." He glowered as I unlocked the cuffs.

He swung his feet over the bed and stood. He tensed and muttered something, causing her hair to go back to her natural color.

"Come on." Ada took his hand and ignored his attempts to pull it free. "Let's go get that Sharpie off your forehead."

"Sharpie?" He rubbed his forehead and looked at his fingertips.

"It won't come off that easily." Ada smacked his arm. "Unless you can magic it off, rubbing alcohol will have to do the trick." The two of them left the room.

"What's the plan today?" Endora sat on the mattress and crossed her legs. "Use me as target practice? Practice voodoo on me?"

"That's not fair." I needed to bond with her, but I wasn't sure how. "We don't want to hurt you."

"Just kidnap me and cut me off from the world?" She huffed and stared out the window. "What do you want from me?"

"For you to be part of our family." Even Logan and Gabby felt like they were part of my family now. Because of our pack link, they were, but it went deeper than that. I felt a kinship with each one of these girls and their mates. We'd all been given different challenges to become who we needed to be.

She arched an eyebrow in disbelief. "Against my will?"

"No, she's never done that." Honor hugged me. "She's saved us all and never pushed for us to do anything we didn't want to do."

"Until me." She fell back on her elbows. "Story of my life."

"The whole 'woe is me' thing won't work anymore," Aidan growled. "You tried to hurt my mate, and the only reason I'm not tearing out your throat is because it would upset her."

Emma, Ada connected with the pack's mind link. *We need you in the family room.*

I'd never heard her sound like that before. "Let's hurry."

I rushed to her with the others right behind me.

"Is something wrong?" Endora asked as she followed us.

In the living room, the mattresses had already been put away, and the rest of the pack wasn't here. Sunny lounged on the couch, but distress flowed through our bond. My heart froze when I took in Finn's pale face.

He faced me with Ada by his side. Ada held a white paper towel soaked with rubbing alcohol, but there weren't any ink stains. He must have used magic since the writing was gone without a trace.

Finn's neck tensed, and a vein bulged. "I received a message from The Hallowed Guild."

"Okay." I didn't think he'd want to remind me that he'd been working with our enemy behind our back.

"They demanded to know where you are." He licked his lips. "Now that they've learned how many of you there are and that all the girls have been found, they're getting desperate."

"Spit it out," Ada growled, "or I will."

"You didn't tell them, did you?" Aidan said with rage.

"God, no." Finn took a step back. "I realized I was wrong, and I haven't been talking to them, but they sent me a text on the phone they gave me."

"Oh my God." Ada snatched the phone from him and tossed it to me. "Just look."

Now that you aren't helping us anymore, the blood of your race is on your hands. We'll start with the Alpharetta coven.

"Why would they tell us that?" Honor scratched her head.

"Because they want you to show up," Endora jutted out her hip. "Which I'm assuming you will do, but if you don't, they'll still win. Fewer abominations in the world."

"We can't allow them to attack a coven for no reason." I couldn't live with myself if we didn't help. *Sunny, call Eric and see what he knows.* "Where is this going down?"

My gut told me that both Aidan's and Barry's packs were involved.

Sunny pulled her phone from her pocket.

Not here. As much as I wanted to trust Endora, she had to earn it. *I don't want Eric to be found out.*

Got it. Sunny opened the front door and called over her shoulder, "Be back in a minute."

"I'll alert the others." We needed to get a move on. They'd only messaged Finn minutes ago, so hopefully, we'd have time to get there since it was only two hours away. *Guys, head back here. We need to go.*

What's going on? Gabby asked.

A coven is under attack, and they need our help. The witches were as much our people as the shifters, and they deserved our protection.

Where is everyone? Aidan asked.

We're out for a run. Ivory sounded happy. *It's been a while since I've run for enjoyment.*

It did sound nice. *I'm sorry, but we need to head out.*

We're on our way. Logan sounded energized. *I'm looking forward to taking out some shifter assholes.*

That sounded about right. *Okay, just make sure you're clothed before coming up here.* Honor snorted even though she paced the room. *I don't need to see any dangling bits.*

Speak for yourself, Beth chimed in. *I haven't gotten any for a while, so I should at least see what everyone is working with.*

Ada placed her arm through Finn's, and he closed his eyes like he enjoyed her touch.

I linked with Aidan. *Is something going on with those two?* We'd been running around like crazy, and Ada was still new here. This had to be a recent development.

Looks like it. Aidan paced around the coffee table. "Finn, do you mind getting Beatrice? We should be on the same page."

"Yeah." He stepped away from Ada and popped his fingers. "Thanks for that." He spun on his heel and rushed to the door.

Ada watched him walk out the door. "You know, he's not so bad."

Endora waved a hand. "He attacked me this morning."

"After you attacked his cousin." Ada lifted a hand. "I mean, she is his only family."

"Right now, this isn't important." We could save this conversation for later.

Sunny linked to the whole pack. *Just hung up with Eric. The five packs are on the move. Everyone is being called to Mount Juliet. They're preparing for war.*

Did Eric know anything about today? I hated to doubt Finn, but I needed to make sure his story checked out.

Yes. While they wait for the packs to get closer, Barry's and Maverick's packs are heading to the Alpharetta coven. Sunny entered the house as she pocketed the phone. *There will be around seventy-five shifters. They're hoping we'll show up, so we need to be strategic. Eric said they're going to attack before nightfall to throw the witches off guard. They're meeting up in Kennesaw.*

They'd picked a location close to Kennesaw, Athens, and not too long of a drive from Mount Juliet.

"Aidan, can you talk to Beatrice when she gets here?" *I need to warn Jacob.*

Aidan winced. *That's not something I wanted to hear.*

I'm calling Mom. I didn't want Jacob to have my number in case Prescott got a hold of it. *I'll be right back.* I walked out back and dialed Mom's number.

"Hey, baby girl," she said happily. "I didn't expect to hear from you so soon."

"I wish it was under better circumstances, but I'm worried about Jacob." I got to the point immediately. "Is he back at campus?"

"No, he's not." Mom cleared her throat. "After the game in Kentucky, he decided to go back to the local community college."

"Thank God." That was one thing going our way. "His roommate's pack is heading to Crawford, and I didn't want him to get caught in the crossfire again."

"I told him you care about him," Mom said proudly. "It's not the way he wants you to, but you love him."

"You're right, I do, but only as a friend." I'd never cared for him as more than that. I'd been lying to myself by thinking I could move on from Aidan.

"You sound happy now, and that's all that matters to me."

"I love you." She had been a mother to me when she didn't have to be.

"Love you too."

"I'll call you soon." I hung up the phone right as Logan, Gabby, Ivory, Remus, and Beth walked out from the woods.

"What's the plan?" Beth pulled on her shirt.

"Not sure yet." I opened the door and waved them through.

Inside the house, I could smell that Beatrice and the rest were there.

Samuel sat on the couch between Amethyst and Coral while Beatrice paced behind them. Rowan sat in the recliner that faced the kitchen while Sage, Aidan, Endora, Honor, Beth, Ada, and Finn sat at the kitchen table.

"How many do you think should go with you?" Beatrice traced her lips. "There are about seventy witches there."

Remus walked over to the kitchen table and sat in the chair facing the living room. "The Hallowed Guild won't have planned for that many."

"Why?" Most covens we'd come across had around fifty to a hundred members.

"Because we've purposely downplayed our numbers." Sage stood then propped her back against the wall. "Most people think witches live in covens of thirteen, but for the most part, it's not true. After what happened to the original witch and others after her, we learned we needed bandwidth to live together and protect one another."

"That's one reason we help other covens even if they aren't tied to our own." Amethyst lifted her head. "We're all sisters in the Goddess's eyes."

"Don't try to sound better than what you—" Endora

stopped mid-sentence as her eyes locked on Honor's mark. "You have the mark too."

What do I say here? Honor linked with us in a panicked tone.

"Yes, she does." It was time to tell her. We couldn't leave her behind, so we needed her to connect with us and want to fight beside us. "In fact, we all do." I pointed to Honor, Sunny, Ivory, Gabby, and then me.

"That's what Dad thought, but you didn't have marks that night." She swallowed and pulled at her ear.

"We hid them." I wanted to explain everything to her, but determining a plan was more important. "I'll tell you everything on the way to the coven."

She's coming with us? Logan shook his head. *That's not a good idea.*

What else can we do? We couldn't leave her here. *She's one of us, and she needs to know it. Besides, if she stays, she might wind up manipulating a witch or worse. Keeping her close is our best option.*

We'll keep her with us. Aidan touched the center of my back. *So, none of you have to worry.*

"If they have seventy coven members, I don't think we need to take too many of our own." Beatrice rocked on her feet and clutched her pentagram necklace. "But I'd hate to leave them without enough fighters."

"There are other nearby covens." Rowan picked at her nails. "They'll offer help too. We need to call them all and inform them of what's happening."

"If that's the case, I think the eleven of us"—I motioned to the shifters—"should go. No one else needs to."

"We're going too," Coral said and held her head high. "Amethyst, Samuel, and I have been with you since the beginning. You don't get to leave us behind."

"And me." Finn stepped toward me and touched my arm. "Please. I messed up before, and I get it now. I want to be part of the fight."

I wanted to say "okay," but he could be playing us. "No, I'm sorry."

"She's right, Finn," Beatrice said sternly. "You were helping those wolves, and they're angry. We can't risk something happening to you."

I hoped to be like her one day. She'd managed to tell him no while being nice about it.

"We need to get going." The longer we took to get there, the higher the chance The Hallowed Guild would already have attacked.

Samuel hugged his mother and walked to the front door. He took the two Suburban keys from the key chain holder and tossed a set to Aidan. "Let's roll."

"I'll call them now." Beatrice picked up her phone off the coffee table and tapped the screen. "You all, please be safe. We can't risk losing any of you."

"We will." Amethyst hugged her, and our group headed out. The mated couples and Endora took one vehicle while the three witches, Beth, Ada, Sunny, and Honor took the other vehicle.

Endora sat in the very back and scooted close to the side of the car to gain distance from Ivory. "You realize they won't stop now until every single one of us is dead."

Gabby snorted. "And you thought we were all rainbows and unicorns."

"We're aware of what they want." I'd hoped my life would change once I got to college, but I hadn't prepared for this. I wouldn't change a thing since it had led Aidan back to me, but there was a lot left to be desired. "But we can't let that happen."

"Why not?" Endora asked with true curiosity, not with malice.

"How you were treated growing up wasn't right." It was that simple.

"And I grew up in The Hallowed Guild." Aidan glanced in the rearview mirror. "And how they treat women isn't okay."

"Wait ... you're one of us—I mean them." Endora shifted in her seat and rolled her shoulders. "You don't act like it."

"How so?" Aidan winked at me, helping me with my cause. *We'll get her there.*

With him by my side, I had no doubts.

"You're very loving and attentive." Endora glanced out the window at the trees flying by.

"Does it surprise you that we're from a Hallowed Guild pack too?" Ivory laid her head on Remus's shoulder.

"My brother, Prescott, is nice like you two." Endora rubbed her hands together. "He's how I survived."

I wanted to laugh, but she was being sincere. "Really?"

"He helped me a lot and took responsibility for some of my mess-ups." She smiled tenderly. "I'll never be able to repay him."

My phone rang, startling me. I answered it and said, "Hello?"

"We have ten members from two other nearby covens coming to help," Beatrice said, cutting to the chase. "So, a total of twenty. Do you think that will work?"

"We'll make it work." I took Aidan's hand in mine. "We have to."

CHAPTER FOURTEEN

I t had been two hours, and if the thickening trees were
any indication, we were getting close to the coven. We
followed behind Samuel, allowing the witches to lead
the way.

Beth connected to us. *We'll circle around for a few
minutes to watch for anything out of the ordinary.*

*Sounds good, but if they're smart, we won't find anything
odd.* It wouldn't hurt to look around, though.

I take it the coven hasn't been attacked yet. Aidan
scanned the area for signs of his father.

No, we wouldn't be driving around if they had, Ada
replied unhappily.

She couldn't be pissed that we hadn't allowed Finn to
come, surely? *Are you okay?*

Finn should've come. Ada's annoyance pulsated through
the bond. *He's the only reason we'll get there in time.*

You don't know what he's been like, Beth snapped. *He
hasn't been the most welcoming, and the more shifters we
found, the angrier he got. He was working with The
Hallowed Guild, for fuck's sake.*

But he was trying to make it up by telling us, Ada responded. *You should've seen how nervous he was about it, but he didn't hesitate to let you all know.*

She's right, Sunny said, siding with Ada. *I was there, and he didn't pause.*

Don't forget he attacked Endora. Gabby's dislike saturated each word. *But I guess that's okay with you.*

He did it because she tried to hurt his cousin, Ada snapped. *How would you feel if someone attacked your family member?*

We wouldn't know, Logan growled, protecting his mate from the small dig. *Did you forget we don't have the privilege of having family?*

That's a blessing. Ada didn't hold back. *At least you weren't beaten by your lowlife father each day.*

Things were escalating, and I needed to get a handle on it before we imploded. *Now isn't the time to question my decisions. We can discuss it further later. Right now, no one dies on our side, including us.*

Fine, Ada agreed begrudgingly.

We drove around in circles for half an hour, stopping at each side road to look for vehicles, but we never found anything. After circling a second time, Beth linked back to us. *We're heading there now.*

We turned onto a dirt road not traveled often. Not even half a mile in, we hit bumps in the ground. I'd learned not to be surprised. Covens tended to live more remotely than even the shifters, likely due to the witch trials that'd taken place over the centuries.

Honor's voice popped into my mind. *We'll stop while they take the perimeter down.*

Our vehicles idled while we waited to pull through.

"If they have a perimeter up, how can the Hallowed Guild actually attack them?" Ivory asked.

"My father is crafty," Endora spoke strongly, and her face turned a shade lighter. "He doesn't mind dabbling with witches who utilize black magic."

"Whoa ..." Remus sounded scared. "You're saying an influential member of The Hallowed Guild uses witches?"

"They hate white-magic witches more than the society does." Endora shivered. "One saw my mark and almost cursed me right then and there. Dad told her to back off, that I was his for a purpose."

I was sure she was, and considering how she'd acted when she'd seen him, it made me nervous. I only knew she needed to leave with us at the end of the night, no matter what. On the bright side, we might have gotten a strategic advantage.

Three witches appeared in front of the road and motioned for us to drive through.

As we pulled into the neighborhood, it struck me how much nicer theirs was than others. Around seventy-five two-story, brick houses came into view. The woods surrounded them protectively, but beyond that, it was modern. They even had a clubhouse at the center of the grassy community lot, which backed up onto a wide-open field where they likely conducted their magic.

A large group was already gathered in the center, and Samuel headed right toward them and parked in the small lot outside the community building. We pulled up beside them, and our group clambered out of the vehicle.

The three witches caught up to us. The taller grayish-haired man headed to us and shook our hands. "We appreciate each one of you for coming out." He thrust his scrawny chest as he shook my hand, his charcoal eyes meeting mine. "And you're one of the prophesied ones."

Each time we met a witch, we received a similar reaction. They placed so much hope on us that it was daunting at times. If we failed, the repercussions would be costly.

"Yes, and these five"—I pointed to each one of us—"are the chosen as well."

"There are six of you?" His face twitched. "I thought there was only one for each side of the pentagram."

"So did we." Beth leaned back on the vehicle. "But, oh well."

The rest of the group introduced themselves, and afterward, he walked us to the large group. An older lady broke away and strolled toward us, her long gray hair and light yellow dress blowing behind her. Her sapphire eyes landed on Amethyst, and she opened her arms wide. "It's been a while, my child."

Amethyst hugged her tight. "At least, at the January gathering, we'll have new witch inductees."

"Very true." The lady turned toward us. "I'm April, Priestess of this coven. We appreciate you coming here to help us in the battle. Caleb, one of our youngest witches, is getting the other twenty settled in. You are the last ones we were waiting on."

"The Hallowed Guild is coming here because of us," I warned.

"Oh, sweet girl." April patted my arm. "Covens like ours have been under attack for thousands of years. It's an honor to fight beside you."

"We need to shift and check out the area." Aidan slipped into protector mode. "The sooner we can get a read on them coming near, the better."

"They won't break the perimeter spell." The older man straightened his shoulders. "We made it strong."

"We have reason to believe they're using black magic," Gabby sneered.

The older man clutched his chest. "My Goddess."

"Harry, this shouldn't surprise you." April's hands shook. "Even if it's bad news."

"I don't understand." Sunny gazed at the ground. "I thought only the witch who put up the perimeter spell could take it down."

"That's usually the case, but dark witches have the dark one on their side." Coral pursed her lips. "So, they can get through certain spells just as we can get through theirs."

"It's a true light versus evil conundrum." Samuel lifted his head to the sky.

"Either way, we need to get a leg up on them," Remus said, echoing Aidan's sentiment.

"Can someone take down the barrier so we can get out?" I didn't want to do anything that would expose them.

"Actually, here." April pulled out several necklaces with a silver pentagram pendant. "These will let you in and out of the perimeter without any issues as long as you're wearing it."

It reminded me of Beatrice's necklace.

Beth linked with us. *That's a neat trick.*

Yes, it is. Ada's face looked like a kid's on Christmas morning.

"Thanks." I took a necklace from April. "Let's all go out, but Endora stays back with the others. We don't want you to get hurt."

Or run away, Logan grumbled.

Honor took a pendant from the Priestess too. *Saying "hurt" makes it sound a whole lot better.*

"But ..." Endora started but stopped. "Fine."

The others took their necklaces and put them on.

"We shouldn't be too long." Aidan placed his hand in mine, and our group headed to the tree line.

Do you think they're here? Sunny asked anxiously.

Not sure. They knew as much as I did. *At the first whiff, though, we run back to warn the others. No one plays hero.*

Agreed. Aidan squeezed my hand. *We only need to know when they get near. If they catch the coven off guard, that'll be bad.*

Let's shift. Even though our scent would be stronger, it didn't matter. They knew we'd be here. *Girls over here.* I pointed to the left.

Our group split into two, and my wolf clawed in anticipation. She hadn't been out in several days, and she wanted to run in the woods. I'd rather it be for pleasure, but it was something.

I stripped down to my birthday suit and let my wolf surge forward. Fur sprouted across my arms as my bones crunched and my body shrank to all fours. My vision sharpened even more, and I dug four paws into the ground, running toward the men.

The girls ran behind me, and the men stood where we'd left them to wait for us.

Is everyone ready? I examined everyone to make sure they had their necklaces on.

They nodded, so I took off deeper into the woods.

In a few steps, the vibration of the perimeter energized the air. The magic didn't feel foreign to me any longer. I winced as I trotted toward it, expecting to bounce off the barrier like I'd done before, but there wasn't even friction.

Holy shit. Beth laughed through our bond. *It worked.*

That was pretty cool, Ada agreed as we bounded through the trees.

Make sure not to lose your necklace, or you won't be able to get back through. Aidan wasn't amused like the others. *Stay on high alert.*

The seriousness of the situation settled back amongst the group.

Let's split up. We'd cover more ground that way. *Aidan, Beth, and I will go left. Ivory, Remus, and Ada go straight. The rest of you go right.*

Aidan paused. *Remember, at the first sign that anything is off, let us know immediately.*

Got it. Logan nodded and ran off.

Our group split apart, and silence filled the air. Animals scurried around but more frantically than usual. They could tell something wasn't right around here.

The trees were thick, and the humidity made breathing a challenge. I pushed through the discomfort and listened for anything odd or telling. Beyond the normal thrumming, there wasn't anything out of place.

Everything good so far? I needed to check in and make sure nothing strange had happened.

We're good here, Gabby answered.

Same here, Ada replied.

Silence filled the bond again. The trickling of a stream could be heard faintly in the distance.

I could use a drink, Beth complained. *It's so damn hot for this time of year.*

We should be there soon. It wouldn't hurt to take a quick break and scan our surroundings.

Minutes later, we were approaching the stream when an uncomfortable cold chill tickled my spine. It felt similar to when Aidan and Bradley had been watching me at

Crawford. Even though I hadn't been able to see him, I'd known he was there.

Beth ran over to the stream and lapped the water.

Aidan tensed and scanned the area. *Is something wrong?*

I ... I think so. The sensation grew colder in warning. *Let's get outta here.*

Something rustled several feet away from us, and Beth went still.

Run! Aidan screamed.

We can't leave Beth behind. I stayed in place, watching Beth run in our direction. *Everyone, get back to the coven. They're here.*

Are you safe? Ivory's voice shook.

Yes. Just get back. Aidan's voice strained. *We can't smell or hear them. Emma felt like we were being watched.*

They had to know we were near. Honor's hesitation flew through the bond. *Maybe we should come help.*

No, they'll catch you. We needed everyone to get back to safety. *Go. We'll let you know if we need help.*

When Beth had almost reached us, a tree limb broke and slammed into her side, launching her into the air. She hit the ground hard and whimpered.

Beth. I rushed toward her. A strong gust of wind blew underneath me, lifting me into the air. The air reminded me of a greasy pan. The more I moved, the more I was covered in disgusting filth.

Emma! Aidan exclaimed. *Jump.*

I tried to lower myself to gain some traction to jump, but my legs wouldn't move. I was at the mercy of whatever held me.

If I wanted to get out of this, I had to focus on what I'd

learned. I closed my eyes as a sluggish buzzing similar to the witches' magic held me. That's when it hit me.

This had to be black magic.

The wolves aren't attacking us. It's the witches. The realization sat heavy in my stomach. *You need to let the coven know.*

I'm okay. Beth stood and rushed back to me. Beth gawked next to Aidan as they tried to figure out how to save me.

The wind lifted me higher and moved me toward where the witches had to be hiding.

We have to get her down. Aidan jerked his head from side to side. *I think I've got it.* He ran toward a tree that had a dent in the base of the trunk. He jumped right at the section and used his legs to propel himself toward me.

A gust of wind blew through me and right into him, knocking him back to where Beth stood.

A loud evil laugh echoed all around us. "Did you really think that would work?" A woman dressed in all black appeared out of thin air. Loose sections of her braided black hair blew across her face, and her dark, soulless eyes seemed dead. "Oh, right, you can't talk."

I tried breaking away from the hold on me, but it tightened, squeezing the breath out of me.

When I hovered right in front of her, she tapped a finger on her bottom lip and tsked. "How pathetic you are."

It pissed me off that I was in wolf form. If I'd been human, I could have at least told her where to go.

Aidan howled as he tried breaking through whatever blocked him from me.

"Don't worry." The witch turned her finger in a circle, and the wind followed the direction. Soon, I hung upside down in the air. "I won't hurt you. I'm just here to help out a business partner."

My necklace fell down my face as it dangled.

She reached out and snatched it. "I'll take that." She then flicked her hand toward Aidan and Beth, and the wind guided me toward them, turning me back around.

The girl disappeared behind the trees, and I dropped to my feet five feet from Aidan and Beth.

Are you okay? Aidan ran at the barrier again and made it through. *Did she hurt you?*

Heart racing, I linked with the entire pack. *No, she took my necklace. That's what she came for. Now they have a way past the perimeter. Let the witches know.*

CHAPTER FIFTEEN

The three of us rushed back to the coven. I ran in the middle. I hated needing protection, but if I complained, they'd team up on me, so I kept my mouth shut.

Soon, we heard wolves running our way. I linked with the others, and my body stiffened. *Crap, there are more coming.*

No, it's us, Gabby replied. *You seemed to be in trouble.*

She actually sounded worried. At least it showed they were coming around, albeit slowly. *We're good. Just rushing back to the coven.*

Speak for yourself, Beth complained. *My side hurts from how that bitch witch threw me.*

Bitch would've worked, Ada interjected.

I liked how it rhymed, Beth grumbled. *Leave the injured person alone.*

Guys, we need to focus, Aidan said briskly. *In only a few hours, The Hallowed Guild is going to attack us.*

Leave them alone. We'd all gone through so much shit.

They need time to decompress. No one is attacking us yet, so let them blow off some steam.

You're right. He huffed beside me. *It's just I could've lost you again. I couldn't get to you, and it hurt to know that there was nothing I could do.*

If I'd seen him in a similar situation, I'd have felt the same way. To watch someone you love get caught couldn't be easy. *But nothing happened, and I'm here with you.*

Aidan bared his teeth and increased his speed. *That doesn't make it better. We got lucky again. One day, our luck might run out.*

We ran down a hill and found Gabby, Logan, Sunny, and Honor waiting at the bottom. They turned back in the direction they'd come from and ran slower, waiting for us to catch up.

Extra back-up wouldn't hurt. Logan flanked Beth while Gabby flanked Aidan.

Agreed. Aidan sounded relieved.

For the next several minutes, the only sounds we heard were the pounding of our paws and animals scurrying.

They're clearing out, Logan said with concern. *That's what happened after my father was killed and the new alpha took over.*

Wait ... your father was the alpha? He'd known about The Hallowed Guild when we'd found him, but he'd kept silent about his past and his knowledge. Remus and Aidan normally led the charge on knowledge.

Yeah, he was until the current alpha murdered him. Agony wafted off from Logan. *I was only five years old, and the coward snuck in and severely injured Dad before challenging him. He knew I was the alpha heir since the eldest was a girl; my sister was eight, so he acted before I could beat him. When I became stronger, he wed my sister and used her as leverage over me. He gave me this scar right before he rejected me and pushed me away.*

And it worked. No wonder he was so angry. I'd be lashing out at everyone too. The Hallowed Guild had done so many wrongs.

When I attacked him for beating her, he had one of his betas bring her out with a noose around her neck. His voice cracked. *They told me to leave or they'd kill her. She's the only family I have.*

You did the right thing, Gabby said with so much love it broke my heart. *And when this is over, you'll take your place as alpha of your pack. We'll kill that asshole and his cronies for what they did to you.*

The trees thinned out as we approached the coven, but we'd learned so much in the past two hours: Logan's real story, The Hallowed Guild had a black magic witch aiding them, and we had to prepare for a battle.

She's right. That was the missing link. We had a connection to each pack of The Hallowed Guild: Aidan to the original pack, Remus and Logan who were the alpha heirs, Eric the current alpha, and Endora to Barry's pack. This had to be a strategic part in the original witch's plan. *We'll make sure you get justice.*

Of course, he'd be opening up now. Aidan sounded amused. *It makes sense, though. He's most comfortable in bad situations.*

True. We were back where we'd changed before the run, and Beth, Gabby, Sunny, Honor and I ran to our clothes. It took a minute for us to return in human form fully clothed.

As we met back with the guys, a little fact knocked me on my ass. "I can't go back in there." I pointed to my bare neck. "I don't have a necklace."

"I'll go get one for you." Beth headed to where we'd come from, passing through the perimeter with no issue.

"There was no indication that a witch was there?" Gabby paced the area, looking behind the surrounding trees.

"No, she must have used a spell or something." Finn's parents had hidden themselves, and my dad had too when they'd dropped me off at the Rogers pack border. My dad had died right beside me as the two witches had snuck back out. They'd dropped the spell too soon because the wolves had found them before they could get very far.

"That's one reason The Hallowed Guild teaches us not to trust witches. They can hide themselves and their evil intentions while remaining undetected." Aidan rubbed his eyes. "Yet, they're working with the worst of that kind."

"Are you surprised?" Logan cracked his neck. "They're willing to do whatever it takes to stay on top."

"They know if we succeed, their whole structure will get challenged." *Opportunists* described them perfectly. They only cared about getting ahead or staying in control.

"Damn sexist assholes." Gabby rolled her shoulders. "It's amazing how you two and Remus turned out okay."

"Don't forget Eric." We'd only said a few words to him, but he'd been just as instrumental in helping us navigate the messy society.

Gabby stretched, limbering up for the unavoidable. "He did almost kill Sunny."

"True, but he didn't." Aidan took my hand. "And that means something. He risked his life to save her."

Beth linked as she stepped between houses, heading our way. *You guys still okay?*

Yeah. I tried not to sound short, but things were getting

intense. We needed to discuss our plans before The Hallowed Guild got here.

Beth tossed the spare necklace to me, and I almost dropped it. I clutched it to my chest and hurried toward the perimeter. The more time we wasted, the more imminent the situation would become.

We walked between the two houses that backed against the woods, and in the center of the grassy field, the group of witches had multiplied. The tension in their bodies was evident from where we stood.

"Thank God, you're okay." Amethyst rushed over and wrapped her arms around me. "They said a witch of black magic took your necklace."

"How did you know it was mine?" Her empath abilities freaked me out at times.

"Because Beth said you needed a spare necklace." Amethyst tried to hide her amusement by mashing her lips together.

Coral placed an arm around her shoulders. "She's good, but not that good."

"I can't believe they have a witch using black magic." April wrung her hands.

"We need to put up a new perimeter spell before it gets too late." I didn't know much about magic, but that I knew.

A wolf howled not far away.

"It's too late for that," Harry said and then shouted, "Get the rest! It's time we prepare!"

A few more men and women ran from the houses toward us.

"Do you have any children here?" Protecting the innocents was most important.

"A few of the older teenagers took them into town."

April straightened her back. "We won't allow our young's blood to be spilled. They are the future of this coven."

"They're ten miles away, tops." Aidan waved his hand, encompassing the neighborhood. "They'll surround us, so we need to spread out along the tree line. The longer we can hold them off outside the neighborhood, the more we'll weaken them and have a fighting chance."

The group dispersed, and I grabbed Endora's hand, making her come with us. *Everyone, spread out among the witches.* We could communicate easily whereas the witches didn't have a bond as we did. If one side got into trouble, we could alert each other. *We'll take the entrance to the neighborhood.* I had a feeling that's where the big dogs would come in. They would want to be seen front and center like the egotistical assholes they were.

Okay! Sunny responded as they split up into groups of two. The couples ran off together, then Sunny and Beth, and finally Honor and Ada.

"You need to stay close at all times." I sounded like a tyrant, but my options were limited.

"But ..." Her eyes darted around the area, searching for someone.

I had a hunch who it was, and she wasn't going back to her father even if it killed me. I kept my grip secure on her arm, forcing her to keep up.

What do you think will happen when Barry and Prescott see her? Aidan ran slightly ahead of us.

No clue. Prescott had been an asshole, so the loving, doting brother she'd described didn't resonate. *I bet her father won't be thrilled, but we need to be careful. Victims tend to go back to their abusers.*

Then, why did we bring her? Aidan growled.

Because if we left her behind with the witches, something

bad would happen. She'd grown up hating them. *She's safer with us.*

I hope you're right. But if something happens to you because of her ...

If something happens to either her or me, the game is over. He had to comprehend that. *They win.*

Silence descended among us as we reached the edge of the subdivision. I slowed and allowed Endora to stand between Aidan and me. We both had to keep an eye on her.

Displeasure rolled off him in waves, but he didn't make a move.

Amethyst appeared on my other side with Coral standing between her and Samuel. April stood on Aidan's other side, and we all stared down the road.

Another howl sounded closer than the last. They weren't hiding the fact they were closing in.

We stood side by side, breathing rapidly and waiting for the inevitable.

"There's no way the perimeter will hold?" The protection would've been a godsend.

"No," Amethyst tapped her fingers on her leg. "The witch was able to replicate the coven's signature magic. She probably dispersed it to each shifter. They'll run in here without issue."

Barry and Prescott stepped through the tree line while Maverick and Bradley came from the right side of the road. Prescott was dressed in his usual preppy style with a tan button-down shirt tucked into his khaki pants. His light brown hair was short, and his light brown eyes landed right on his sister.

The look of disgust was clear on Maverick's face. He wore jeans and a shirt, matching Aidan's casual style, but between that and his dark hair, that's where the similarities ended. The older man had crow's feet but was muscular like his sons. His dark hair was short with gray peppered throughout, but his eyes weren't golden. They were icy green.

The ever-obedient son, Bradley, walked right behind him. He looked similar to Aidan, but he was a tad less built, and his eyes were a dark honey. He had the usual scowl on his face until his gaze landed on Endora. His brows furrowed as he continued to stare.

They met in the middle of the road that led to the neighborhood and turned, heading straight toward us.

The alphas walked a few steps in front of their alpha heirs.

Sneering, Maverick stopped fifty feet away. "Well, well. Why am I not surprised my traitor son is here?" He lifted his right hand, showing us a huge ring on his middle finger.

"Are you expecting that to upset me?" Aidan lifted his chin and met his father's gaze.

"It should." His father glared at me. "It's interesting you're choosing not to stand by her."

How does he know you aren't? The observation caught me off guard.

Because Bradley is behind him telling him that. Aidan's jaw tensed. *They're messing with us.*

Yeah, I gathered that. I squared my shoulders at Maverick and smiled. "It's nice to meet you ... *Dad.*" I punched the word, trying to get under his skin.

Maverick's face turned a shade of red. "You are not my family."

"She is, though." Aidan smiled adoringly at me. "We've claimed each other after all."

"Do you think this is funny?" Maverick's nostrils flared. "Do you know how damn embarrassing it is?"

"And don't forget they captured my daughter." Barry's hateful gaze landed on Endora. "I should've known she'd turn on me."

"No, Daddy." Endora jerked her head from side to side. "They took me against my will."

"That just means you really wanted to go." Barry pointed at her, wielding his finger like a sword. "You aren't worthy of our pack. You never were."

"Dad, come on," Prescott said, stepping toward his father. "You know she would never—"

"Enough!" Barry shouted. "You are not the alpha, and thank God for that if you want to show her mercy."

"But I tried ..." Endora stopped, her lip trembling.

"Maybe we shouldn't be so hard on her." Bradley winced.

Barry swung around to face Bradley. "Are you telling me what to do?"

Wow, they're almost imploding. Maybe we didn't need to worry.

Don't get comfortable. Aidan flicked his focus to me. *They'll get back on track.*

"No ..." Bradley stuttered. "It's just—"

"He needs to learn to keep his mouth shut." Maverick scowled at his son. "We need to stay on course."

"What do you want?" Whatever they said, it wouldn't happen, but we had to try.

"For you and the abominations to turn yourselves over to us." Maverick spread his arms out wide. "You do that, and all of this ends."

"There's no way in hell she'd ever do that." Aidan clenched his hands at his sides.

"Maybe the witches don't feel the same way you do."

Barry grinned charismatically at the ones standing around us. "You don't want to die for them, so let us take them."

"Do you think we're that stupid?" Laughter laced April's words. "Even if we did, you'd still attack us."

"I give you my word." Maverick placed a hand on his chest. "We won't harm anyone else."

"Our answer is still no." April sucked in a breath. "They're part of our own. There's no way we'd turn our back on them, not the way you have."

"Then you leave us no choice." Maverick's eyes glowed. "Let the games begin."

Loud howls filled the air. It was the sound of war.

CHAPTER SIXTEEN

They'll focus their attack on you and the other marked girls. Aidan linked with the pack. *Everyone, focus on the girls. If something goes wrong, alert us and the witches near you.*

We won't allow them to lay a hand on any of them, Logan rasped.

That's one thing we can agree on, Remus growled.

Fear poured from Beth, and she hid it the only way she knew how. *Anyone else feel an overwhelming level of testosterone spewing off those three?*

I'm feeling tingles in the southern region. Ada snorted. *If I sprout a dick, I won't be happy.*

Whatever. Honor quipped. *You'd be playing with it for days.*

I've always wondered what it would be like to swing one around. Ada's amusement flowed to us all. *Maybe do a little pinwheel action.*

I had to hold back my laughter. It would only encourage them, and Aidan was about to lose it.

The howls ended, and an eerie silence descended.

Now isn't the time for jokes. Aidan's anger was palpable. *They're about to strike. Everybody needs to have their heads in the game.*

An earth-brown wolf ran from the woods, followed by more. As expected, the wolves had spread out in a circle, hoping to catch us unprepared.

Black fur sprouted across Aidan's body as he called his wolf forward. *Stay in human form. We need to be able to talk to Endora, and she'll listen to you more than me.*

I wasn't sure I agreed, but his clothes were already ripping. Good thing we'd brought more clothes as backup. *Okay.*

"Endora, stay right beside me." Now that I'd seen how she looked at her father, I doubted whether we should've brought her. But no matter what we'd decided to do, she was a liability.

"But I want to go back home," she said, her voice breaking at the end.

"We are your home." I wanted to strangle her, but the wolves were within striking distance.

Two wolves from each side ran at us. The right two focused on Endora while the left two were locked on me.

Amethyst lifted her hands as she mumbled words, and a wolf near me flew back in the air.

However, the other three didn't hesitate. They ran full blast, and Aidan jumped in front of us.

You can't fight three at the same time. He'd lost his mind. That was the only explanation.

I'll be fine. He dropped to four legs and hunkered down, baring his teeth.

If you think I'll stand back and let you get hurt, you're in for a rude awakening. We'd all come here to fight.

Samuel rushed to Aidan's side, chanting, his focus on

the one remaining wolf intent on attacking me, freeing Aidan to contend with the two on his side. However, more wolves ran out of the woods.

A wolf reached each witch, thrashing and fighting. It was a battle of wills and concentration. A reddish wolf circled behind his pack members, coming from the left and heading straight toward us. They were masterminding a sneak attack, and no one had noticed but me.

I pretended to be distraught in order to catch him off guard. "Endora, what do we do?"

Her head jerked toward me. "Are you serious right now?"

At least, I had her fooled. "Yeah. Should we run back to the house?" My attention flicked to the alphas and alpha heirs standing in the exact same place. They were specta-tors, letting their minions do their evil work.

Endora blinked but said nothing.

That's when Aidan charged the two reddish-brown wolves. They stumbled. He'd caught them off guard. His teeth sank into one's throat, ripping it out. The wolf fell to the ground, and the thick metallic scent of blood filled the air.

The other wolf jumped on his back and bit into his side.

Aidan, no. I'd moved to help him when he fell onto his back, landing on the wolf. The wolf whimpered and released his hold.

The light brown wolf was only two feet from Samuel. He said some words, and the wolf tripped.

The sneaky reddish wolf's gaze stayed on Samuel, ready to eliminate him. He crept along until he was in the attack zone.

Samuel hadn't noticed the wolf beside him.

It stood on its back legs, its mouth open wide.

I had to act. I spun around and kicked the wolf right in its head, and it tipped over.

"What the...?" Samuel lost focus.

The light brown wolf knocked him over, landing right on top of him. As it snapped at his neck, I steamrolled the wolf off Samuel and pushed it onto its back.

What the hell are you doing? Aidan growled through our mate bond.

Protecting Samuel. I wasn't about to let one of my friends die when I could prevent it.

Aidan rushed over, ripped the wolf's throat out, and stepped over it to help Samuel with the light brown one.

In the second I'd taken my eyes off her, Endora had run through the pack, right toward her father.

"Endora!" I yelled, but she only increased her speed.

The girl couldn't be serious. Who wanted to live like that? I ran toward her, not thinking this whole thing through. If we lost her, it would all be over. They wouldn't stop at one marked girl. They'd take us out one by one. We'd always be hunted.

Coral grabbed my hand. "No. Nothing good can come of it."

"But we need her," I said and yanked my arm out of her hold, but Amethyst clutched my other arm.

Amethyst's eyes darkened to a deep purple, and the bloody scratch marks dripped blood, causing them to stand out even more. "Don't make me hold you in place."

"Oh, my God." I reached out to touch her face but stopped. "Are you okay?"

"It's fine." She wiped the blood from her chin, only for more liquid to replace it. "We need to focus, or we're all going to die."

"Can you get her back?" I asked, turning toward the alphas as Endora reached them.

Her dad sneered at her. "You let me down."

"I'm sorry. I didn't mean to." Her hands shook as she held them out to him. "But I didn't help them."

"You expect me to believe that?" His face twisted with disgust. "You know why I can't trust you." He lifted his hand to slap her, but Prescott caught it.

"Dad, wait." Prescott stepped in front of his sister. "We can use her to our advantage."

My stomach soured at his words.

Prescott motioned to the tree line. "They'll be desperate to get her back. I'll take her in the woods and let everyone see what's going on. It'll give us an advantage."

Bradley stepped in front of Maverick and Barry. "I'll go with him to make sure it works out."

"Fine," Barry grumbled. "Go, but do it fast."

We might have a chance to get her. This might be a setup, but if we all worked together, we could get the advantage.

Ivory's concerned voice linked back. *What do you mean "get her"?*

They have Endora. I left out the fact she'd willingly gone to them. It didn't change a damn thing. *Bradley and Prescott want to upset us so we'll act irrationally.* Like I had been until Coral and Amethyst had knocked some sense into me. *Be careful, but we need her back.*

Got it, Remus replied.

A solid black wolf rammed into my side, tearing me from Amethyst's grip. It pinned me against a tree. The bark tore at my shirt and into my skin, but I pushed past the pain.

It bit into my arm.

Throbbing pain overtook me, but I swallowed the vomit

down. I moved so my right hand was free and punched the wolf in the head over and over again.

Gold eyes appeared behind my attacker, and Aidan bit into the base of the wolf's neck.

The dark wolf whimpered and loosened its jaws enough for me to free my hand.

Once Aidan realized I'd moved, he shoved the wolf against the tree and tore out its throat. He didn't even bother to watch the wolf die as he ran toward me, blood coating his snout. *Are you okay?* He sniffed my arm, smelling my blood.

Yeah, I'm fine. I pointed at the woods. *Bradley and Prescott took off with Endora. We have to get her back.* The witches, Samuel, Coral, and Amethyst were all locked in battle while the two alphas sat back and watched. It was odd. Why were they even here?

Fine, let's go, but we're going to be careful. Aidan trotted into the trees. *Let's follow their scents, but be as quiet as possible. We need to sneak-attack them.*

I hated leaving our friends behind, but they were fighting, and Endora was getting farther and farther away. We had to leave without them. *Got it.* We needed every advantage we could get. I'd get down and crawl on my hands and knees if that'd help. *I'll follow your lead.*

He knew how these packs acted better than I did. All I cared about was that as many of our people survived as possible. Hell, I didn't want to hurt the packs either, but they'd attacked us, not the other way around.

Endora's scent was thick. Not even the smell of blood could hide it. We moved slowly and methodically through the trees. No wolves were near as they'd all stormed the coven.

How is everyone doing? Our group had to stay intact. We couldn't afford to lose anyone.

Doing good. Logan sounded amused. *We're holding our own over here.*

Same here, Remus said with remorse. *I hate killing our own kind, though.*

They don't give a damn about killing any of us. Hate dripped off Logan's every word. *Or killing each other. The fewer of them, the better.*

I'm not sure I'd go that far. Ivory sighed. *I mean, yes, they aren't perfect, but we're still taking lives.*

We're doing okay here too, Beth interjected. There was no sign of her usual happy demeanor. *But it could change at any time. More seem to be appearing.*

Is anyone hurt? Aidan asked.

Just a few scratches, Honor replied. *Nothing major with us.*

Same here, Logan and Remus echoed.

Okay, we're following Endora. Her scent strengthened, meaning we were getting closer. *Let us know if you need anything.*

"Are you planning to kill her?" Bradley sounded like he was only a quarter of a mile away.

"What?" Endora squeaked. "But I didn't mean—"

"Shut up," Prescott rasped. "Is that why you came out here? To kill her?"

The three of them appeared in front of us, and we stopped hiding behind the trees.

Bradley scowled. "I asked first."

"What do I have to do to prove myself?" Endora ran her hands through her hair and wrapped her arms around her waist. "I'm loyal to the cause."

"Why don't you go back to your father and watch the

fight?" Prescott moved so he blocked Endora. "This isn't any of your business."

"Like hell it's not," Bradley growled and lowered his head. "I'm the alpha heir to the original alpha pack."

"And she's my sister." Prescott took deep, ragged breaths. "Which means she's more tied to us."

Maybe we could get her now. They were in a pissing match. Hell, they hadn't even noticed us yet.

I don't know. Aidan hesitated, scanning the area. *We'll have to be fast. Are you sure she'll come with us?*

Maybe. She thought they might kill her. *I think we should be good unless she still has a death wish.*

Before we could move, a wolf growled from their other side.

Prescott stiffened, and he turned toward the intruder. "What are you doing here, Tony?"

The wolf stepped out of the trees, its sandy-blond fur glistening in the lowering sun.

"No, I'll take care of it." Prescott took Endora's arm and moved her behind him. "You go back and fight the coven."

"Your dad thinks you don't have the balls to do it." Bradley chuckled in disgust, but he stepped toward Endora.

"Both of you, stand down." Prescott's head snapped in one direction then the other. "Go back to the others."

"Are you going to kill me?" Endora stepped back, fear etched into her face. "Please don't."

"Endora, stop!" Prescott yelled, but it was too late.

She was far enough away that the wolf launched right at her.

No! I ran toward them, Aidan right by my side.

I was in human form and wouldn't make it, but Aidan surged forward, desperately trying to get to her.

Right before the wolf could reach Endora, Bradley

jumped in front of her, allowing the wolf to latch onto his throat.

Bradley! Aidan screamed through our bond. Right before the wolf could rip out Bradley's throat, Aidan jumped, turning sideways so he landed on the wolf's back, claws extended. Then, he leaned forward and latched onto the sandy wolf's throat.

The wolf gargled as Aidan jerked his head back, killing it immediately. Its jaw slackened, and Bradley fell forward. I caught him before he hit the ground and cradled him in my lap.

Aidan dropped the sandy wolf to the ground with a sickening smack and ran over to me.

"Endora, are you okay?" Prescott ran to his sister and checked her for injuries.

"Yes ... I ... I'm fine ..." she stuttered and fell to her knees next to me.

Blood spilled out from the bite and all down Bradley's neck and shirt and my legs. But I didn't give a damn. Bradley had saved Endora's life, and I had no clue why.

"He bit into his carotid artery." Prescott bent down and checked the marks. "There's so much blood."

Aidan whimpered and licked his brother's face.

"It's okay," Bradley said in a low, raspy voice, the words almost indistinguishable. "I finally understand."

"What do you mean?" I asked on Aidan's behalf.

"She's my fated mate." He coughed and grasped his neck. "I always thought I'd kill her, but I couldn't let her die."

"What? No." Tears dripped down Endora's cheeks and landed on him. "Stay with me."

"I'm sorry." His breathing became labored. "I wish I could, but there is no saving me."

"Shift into your wolf." There had to be a way to save him. "You can heal faster that way."

"I'm too weak to shift." Blood leaked from the corners of his mouth. "Take care of my brother for me," he said, staring right into my eyes. "And keep Endora safe." His body jerked, and his eyes froze in place.

"No!" Endora screamed and beat her hands against his chest.

Aidan's heart-wrenching howl filled the air.

But now wasn't the time for mourning. Now, we had to protect Endora from her brother.

CHAPTER SEVENTEEN

"We need to go," Prescott said frantically. "Dad knows the wolf was killed. He'll send another."

"I ... I don't understand." Endora wiped the tears from her eyes. "Why would he jump in front of me?"

"Because he protected you from your father." This had to open her eyes ... surely. "The man you love so much wants to kill you and doesn't give a damn who has to die to make it happen."

Aidan shook his head and focused on Prescott. *I'm going to kill him.* He bared his teeth and growled at the alpha heir.

"Look, I didn't want him to follow me." Prescott lifted a hand. "I planned on getting you here and us leaving with you."

"Us?" That didn't make any sense. "You expected to go with us?"

"When my dad figures out I turned her over to you, it won't go well." Prescott huffed and patted himself on the chest. "I'm going against everything he wants by doing this, but it's the only way I can protect her. He doesn't give a shit about her and always planned on killing her when the day came. That day is today."

Endora sat next to Bradley, rocking back and forth. "You're right." She closed Bradley's eyes and kissed his forehead. "Dad has anticipated this day since my birth." She stood, and her eyes landed on me. "I'm in, but I get to kill my father."

This I hadn't expected. "Right now, we need to protect the coven and go. Once we get home, we can learn the next steps."

Prescott took a step in our direction. "If we hit them hard, we can get out of here soon."

Aidan jumped in front of me. *Don't trust him. This could be a trick.*

"We have no reason to trust you." Endora's stories about her brother replayed in my mind. "You ratted Aidan out at Crawford and beat up Jacob."

"When I realized other girls had the mark too, I thought I could save my sister." Prescott's shoulders sagged. "That's why I came there to scout things out too. We'd expected my sister to be the only one marked, so when another girl was identified, I went to see it for myself. I was wrong." Prescott stared at Bradley's corpse. "But I was just trying to save her."

I couldn't fault him for that. "How do we know we can trust you?" We didn't have time for this, but something kept me here.

"He could be alerting the others, and he's not." Endora turned to me. "He's always protected me. He's trustworthy."

"How do you know he's not alerting the others?" Her pack link was blocked.

"When I saw my dad, the spell broke." She grimaced. "I'm connected to the pack again."

"Is that how we couldn't connect or find you?" Prescott asked.

Do you think he's telling the truth? Aidan questioned.

I'm not sure. There was only one way to learn the truth. "If you come with us, we perform the link-blocking spell on you, and you leave your cell phone behind. I'm not risking another attack."

"That's fine." He placed a hand on his heart. "I promise I won't cause any problems and can help figure out how to end this. My sister's life isn't worth the hate that fills their hearts."

It wasn't a lie; the air smelled crisp and clear.

We need to get the witches to block it sooner rather than later. Aidan faced his brother again, and pain radiated through the bond. *Something must change. All the senseless dying must stop.*

"Fine, but any ideas?" We needed a good distraction. "Is there any way to get the wolves to attack a certain area?"

"Yes." Prescott snapped his fingers. "If I tell them the marked girls are trying to escape, we can direct them to a certain area and take out as many as we can until they're forced to retreat."

I'm not a huge fan of this plan. Aidan's torment rang clear. *We can't use you as bait.*

"Wait." This could work. "We could get them to rush here for us, and the coven could surround them."

You're right. Aidan still wasn't thrilled. *But he would have to pretend to be injured or something.*

"Are you a good actor?" Aidan had a good point. We didn't want his dad to know he was a traitor or more wolves wouldn't come.

"I can get by." Prescott pulled his sister into his arms. "I've had to cover for her plenty of times, so I'll be good."

A small sob left her. "I can't believe how messed up this is. I lost my mate and my father on the same day."

I bit back the words I wanted to say. The truth would only make things worse. "Where should we do this?"

Let's get farther from the alphas. Aidan nodded his head in the opposite direction than we'd come from.

I linked with the entire pack. *How is everyone doing?*

Okay. Honor spoke first, which wasn't the norm. *A few witches are hurt, though.*

Same here, Gabby joined in. *But nothing too horrible. We're holding them.*

One witch has died here. Ivory's voice cracked. *The number of wolves is thinning, but they're still attacking strong.*

Let's meet in the woods. I wouldn't bring up Aidan's brother dying. We could tell them later. *We're about a mile east of the road. We're going to run for another half a mile in that direction. Come meet up with us and bring as many witches as possible.*

What's the plan? Beth asked.

We're going to lure the wolves in and surround them. Aidan focused on the task ahead. *Be discreet, and tell the witches the plan. Make sure the wolves can't hear you.*

Uh ... how the hell are we supposed to do that? Logan asked sarcastically.

Draw a picture if you have to. Aidan raged. *I don't give a fuck, just get it done.*

Well, okay then, Ada deadpanned. *We'll be there soon.*

"I'll grab Coral, Amethyst, and Samuel." We couldn't leave them out of the plan. They were part of our team.

No, I'll do it. I can run faster in this form. Aidan brushed his body against my leg. *Be careful.* He took off running.

"Where's he going?" Endora sniffed.

"He wanted to go get Coral, Amethyst, and Samuel instead of me doing it." I forced myself to move in the opposite direction. "Let's hurry."

The three of us ran at a solid clip. The wolves weren't focused on what was going on behind them; their attention was on the enemy in front of them. We stayed deep enough in the tree line so we wouldn't be visible for any enemy searching for a new target.

Aidan

MY HEART FELT FRACTURED. My brother and I had been close when we were younger. He was two years older than me and the heir to lead the pack. Things had been great back then. We'd play fight as wolves. We'd lain with Mom as she'd read us our bedtime stories, and we'd dream about how we'd never allow the curse to ruin our lives. But the night before I turned fourteen, I'd won a fight against him, showing my wolf was more dominant than his.

He'd freaked out and demanded another fight. I should've let him win, but my wolf wouldn't allow it. Not only had I beat him once that night but twice. His pride had been wounded, and he'd looked at me with pure hatred. I'd assured him I would never tell anyone. Dad was so hard on him, I didn't want that for myself, but it didn't matter. Him knowing I could win against him had forced a permanent wedge between us.

The more I'd tried, the more I'd pushed him further away.

I forced myself to stop. By obsessing over my regret, I

was letting myself lose focus on what was going on now, which meant Emma could get hurt. I couldn't live without her.

The trees thinned, and Dad and Barry came back into sight.

"My son better not be hurt." Maverick shoved a finger in Barry's face. "If your son did something ..."

"Prescott is telling me he's fine." Barry's face turned red. "Are you calling him a liar?"

At least, this made me feel more comfortable in trusting the prick. I turned my attention on Amethyst, who must have felt me because her gaze went straight to me.

Her empath skills came in handy. I pawed at the ground and jumped on my front paws. I didn't want to catch my father's attention.

She turned around and moved her hands, blowing at a wolf Coral and Samuel were fighting twenty feet away. It hit a tree. Then, she touched their arms and motioned for them to follow her.

Our group ran behind the witches, staying out of direct sight of the enemies, making it not as apparent that they were running into the woods. Right as they turned toward the woods, a dark blue car came barreling down the road where the alphas stood and fought.

Everyone stopped fighting and turned in that direction, and the three witches ran as hard as they could into the trees.

That car had been the perfect distraction. For once, it felt like fate might actually be on our side.

The four of us ran to join the others. I ran in front, leading the way and listening for any signs of attackers. I had to get back to Emma and fast.

Emma

It didn't take us long to run half a mile east, and the three of us stood in a circle, our backs touching. If someone caught our scent, they could try to surprise us. I tapped into my wolf, keeping attention in case people headed our way.

Paws and footsteps grew closer.

Is anyone near the meeting spot? I tensed, ready to spring into action in case it was an enemy wolf.

Yes, we're almost there. Sunny sounded tired. *We got five witches to follow us.*

Beth, Sunny, and the five witches stepped into view. There was an older, gray-haired man who reminded me of Harry, two middle-aged women, and a man and woman about our age.

The boy, who was maybe a year or two older, focused on Endora. He had shoulder-length, mahogany hair that contrasted with his white shirt. He placed his hands into his jeans pockets as his ebony eyes fixated on the hybrid. He approached her. "Are you hurt?"

"No," Endora replied breathlessly.

Okay, that was strange. More rustling came from the trees.

Ada linked with me. *The rest of us are here. No reason to be alarmed.*

"The others are almost here." I hoped this wasn't a bad plan, but it was too late now. "Did anyone follow you?"

"No. They're locked in battle with the others. The wolves kept running toward the woods and looking back at us, so the ones who could followed."

Aidan, where are you? If something had happened to

him, I wouldn't be as strong as Endora. I'd fall apart, and nothing could put me back together again.

Some of the tension left his voice. *We're almost there.*

Did anyone see you? I watched as the rest of our group appeared in wolf form with another twenty witches.

No. A car came down the road, allowing us to go unnoticed. He sighed. *I was sure my dad would've caught on.*

Well, we have twenty-five witches in total here; the other three will make twenty-eight. This plan might work after all.

Get the wolves' attention and get them headed this way, Aidan said determinedly. *You should be able to hear us now.*

I do. I faced Prescott. "It's time."

"What's going on?" the older man asked and gritted his teeth.

"We're going to direct some of the wolves our way and take them out until they leave." I pointed to Prescott. "He'll tell them there are a few of the marked girls together and he needs some wolves to come help."

"From what I can tell, there's only about fifty wolves left, so if we take down twenty or so of them, they'll retreat." Prescott's attention flicked to the trees as Aidan and the witches walked through.

Aidan ran straight to me and sat next to my feet.

"Are you guys ready to take on some wolves?" I walked over and hugged Sunny, Beth, and Ada, glad to see they hadn't been injured further.

The blood had dried on Amethyst's face, and the scratches seemed more raised.

"We've been worried about you too. You ran off, and we were afraid over the reason." Samuel scanned the group. "Even with the wolf attacks, the witches still outnumber the wolves, so that's a damn miracle."

Prescott stiffened. "Dad's sending twenty our way. They'll be here in two minutes."

"You guys hide." We had to be strategic. "They won't suspect a thing since the scent of witches is heavy around here."

The witches lifted their hands and disappeared from sight. That was freaky as hell.

The shifters created a circle, ready for the first wolf to appear.

It took seconds before the first one drew close.

Prescott stumbled and lifted his hands toward Aidan. "You won't get away with being a traitor," he said angrily. "We're going to kill all of you."

At least, he could play the part well. Three wolves jumped out of the trees, and their attention landed right on me. The gray front one let out a short howl and jumped right at my throat. Logan's silver wolf lunged, bit into the wolf's shoulder, and threw it to the ground.

The next two attacked in succession. Aidan kept his focus on Prescott, maintaining the ruse as Remus and Gabby took on the other two.

Our numbers were good until something shifted inside me. The tingling ran down my back.

"Something's off." I didn't know what, but then the scent of at least forty wolves hit my nose. "They've diverted all of them here."

Prescott must have only known about his pack and not my dad's. Aidan growled as he stopped pretending to fight Prescott. *Everyone, get ready.*

This had been a horrible plan.

I lost count as wolves poured out of the trees to surround us. Snarls and snaps rang loudly in my ears. They all charged at the same time, three coming right at me.

A carrot-colored wolf charged for my throat, and I ducked. It landed on my back, and I spun around and straightened. It flew off me and into the other two only a few feet away.

The witches dropped the veil and helped us.

The attacking wolves weren't fazed. They were intent on taking the wolves out, not sure which ones were marked.

Another one appeared right beside me and sank its teeth into my forearm. I groaned and stuck my fingers into its eyes. At first, there was some resistance, but I pushed until it felt like they were Jell-O.

The wolf wailed as it unlatched and dropped to the ground.

I shook my hand to get rid of the icky feeling. Everyone was holding their own, and a few wolves lay either dead or unconscious. Right when I was about to turn around, I spotted Ada across the clearing, fighting a wolf with her back unguarded.

A wolf tiptoed behind her, ready to lunge.

"Ada!" I yelled, knowing it was futile.

The wolf lunged before she could turn, its mouth wide open.

I pushed my legs as the attack progressed in slow motion. Right as the wolf's teeth were about to sink into the back of her neck, familiar amber hair appeared behind it.

CHAPTER EIGHTEEN

The wolf fell, revealing Ada's savior.

Finn.

Ada stood on her hind legs, knocking the wolf she'd been fighting on its back. She turned around and paused when she saw Finn. *What the hell just happened?*

Pure rage shone on his face as he lifted his hands, murmuring incoherent words.

The wolf she'd dropped was back on all fours. I grabbed a huge branch from the ground and nailed it on the head. *A wolf attacked you from behind, and Finn saved you.*

I turned around in time to see the other wolf fly into a tree and Finn pull out his knife. He lifted it above his head, ran to the wolf, and slammed the knife into its neck. Blood spilled over the handle.

Holy shit. Ada spun around and found the wolf I'd taken care of for her. *You both saved me.*

Let's just say fighting is not your strong suit. I tried to make my tone sound light-hearted, but it fell flat.

I almost died, Ada said in shock. *I can't ...*

Now wasn't the time for her to fall apart. *You're fine. Let's concentrate before you get hurt.*

Finn hurried over to her and placed his hand on her head. "Are you okay?"

"She's fine." I'd never seen him this concerned, especially where a shifter was involved. "A little shaken up, but we have to keep our heads in the game."

A merle-colored wolf bounded toward me and hunkered. I braced for its attack, but it halted and growled before running back toward the alphas.

What the ...

The enemy wolves stopped fighting and followed the merle wolf back to their leaders. I glanced around and found at least ten dead wolves.

Prescott appeared from behind some trees where he'd been hiding.

"Are you fucking serious?" The guy had hidden. The nerve!

"I didn't want dad to know I turned." Prescott motioned to his father. "We need the spell done so he won't know we're with you."

"The spell?" Coral lifted an eyebrow. "Are you talking about blocking the pack link?"

"Yes." Endora held her hand out. "Take my blood and do it."

"Who is this person?" Samuel's head tilted backward. "Is this the same Endora we came here with?"

"No, I'm not." Endora lifted her hand to Amethyst. "You're the strongest of the three, so let's get this done."

"Okay." Amethyst pulled her phone from her pocket. "Let me get the spell from Mom."

"We need to hurry," Prescott pushed. "Dad's calling for me."

Samuel took a step toward Prescott. "Calm down. She's already dialing the number."

I touched Samuel's arm. "He wants to help us."

"Mom?" Amethyst paused. "We're fine, but I need you to send me the pack block spell."

Did you get hurt? Aidan trotted over to me and scanned me.

No. I scratched his head. *I'm fine.*

"Why are you here?" Coral asked as she watched Finn pull the knife from the wolf's neck and wipe the blood off of it onto the wolf's fur.

"I figured you might need backup." He faced Ada. "And I got here in the nick of time."

Coral motioned to the dead wolf. "It didn't have anything to do with killing wolves?"

He glowered at her. "No, actually, it didn't."

"Okay, I've got the spell." Amethyst's phone shook in her hands, and she pulled out a small dagger with the other. "I need a drop of each of your blood in my palm."

"Ew." Samuel's nose wrinkled. "In your hand?"

"Do you have a bowl handy?" she replied. When he didn't say a word, she continued, "I didn't think so."

Endora pricked her finger and held the dagger to Prescott. When he didn't take it, she patted his arm. "It's fine. They've been very nice to me even when I didn't deserve it."

"Fine," he grumbled as he took the dagger and pricked himself. "Hurry."

Amethyst held her hand out, and they dropped their blood. She spoke the words that sounded mumbled.

Crap, the last time we'd done this, a storm had appeared, and lightning had struck inside the house. We should've moved somewhere with cover.

I searched the sky for any sign of a threat, but the darkening sky remained cloud-free.

"It's done." Amethyst lowered her phone. "Do you still feel the link?"

"No." Endora rubbed her hand along her pants. "We're safe now."

"We need to go check on the others." It was imperative to see how many witches had perished. "And bury Bradley's body."

"Who's Bradley?" the young witch asked, surveying our group.

"Aidan's brother." They didn't need to know more than that. "Who the hell are you?"

"Oh, I'm Caleb," he replied sheepishly.

"Are we sure they're done fighting?" The witch closer to our age stared at where the wolves had disappeared. "I'd hate for us to get hurt now that they can't connect with the pack."

"We could hear them coming back." Witches weren't familiar with how our abilities worked just like we weren't sure of theirs.

"And they were leaving." Prescott moved to stand next to Honor. "They were grossly outnumbered and retreated to regroup."

"Will they come back?" I didn't want to leave the pack unattended, but we needed to get back to Beatrice's coven and figure out our next step. I was ready for this to be over.

"No, they won't." Prescott placed his fingers through the loops of his pants. "They know you're going to leave, and more witches might come here. We hadn't expected there to be so many witches even with the warning we gave Finn."

"Either way," the older man said, "we need to check on our own."

"I should be pissed since we told you to stay back." Finn had defied me, but if he hadn't, things would've been worse. "But you saved Ada."

"I'd do it all over again if I had to." Finn touched Ada again. "But I am sorry if I upset you."

"I'm not upset." I patted him on the shoulder and smiled. "But let's not make a habit of it, okay? Now, let's hurry." It was a two-hour drive back to the coven.

Our group made our way back to the houses, and I sighed with relief when I saw the witches huddled in the grassy field with no surrounding threat.

I need to change. Aidan veered right, toward the Suburbans. *Can you help me get clothes from the vehicle?*

Yeah. I touched Amethyst's hand. "Let me go get their clothes so they can shift back, and we can go from there."

She nodded. "Sounds good. We'll be there, waiting for you."

I took the keys out of my pocket and hurried to the Suburban. The wolves followed behind me, and I grabbed the bag with everyone's change of clothes. I placed the bag on the ground and handed out the clothes. The wolves came by, took their clothes in their mouths, and ran into the woods to find a spot to change. Once everyone had been accounted for, I headed back to the others, who were talking with the witches.

"How many did we lose?" That had been weighing heavily on my mind.

A grin spread across April's face. "It's nice hearing a marked one say that."

I wasn't sure how to respond to that.

Amethyst grimaced. "Five witches died."

"But plenty more wolves." Finn motioned to the tree line. Every hundred feet, a wolf was down on the ground, unmoving. I wasn't sure of the tally, but it was much worse than ours.

"The witches died with honor." April pulled her shoulders back. "The Goddess will bestow them with their reward, and we will bury our dead."

Endora wrapped her arms around herself. "Are we going?"

"Not yet." We couldn't leave without personally burying Bradley. Aidan deserved to say goodbye. "Is there a shovel we can borrow?"

"Did someone on your side die?" Harry's gaze flicked over our group. "It looks like you're all here and then some." He stopped at Prescott and frowned.

Couldn't blame him on that one. "No, but my mate's brother died. He deserves to say goodbye before we go."

April lifted a finger. "Wait ... your mate was part of that pack?"

"He's not part of it anymore, but his father was one of the alphas here tonight." I gestured to Endora. "If it hadn't been for Bradley, we would've lost one of our own."

Caleb walked off toward the community building. "I'll go get you a shovel."

The others hurried out from the trees, back in human form.

"What's the plan?" Aidan took my hand and glanced around at the large group. "The night's not getting any younger."

"I know." I stepped closer to his side so our bodies touched. "Caleb is getting a shovel. I figured we'd bury Bradley and the other wolves before we left." I didn't want to leave this coven with the burden of burying the wolves.

"We can bury the other wolves." April turned to her coven. "You take care of your loved one and go. The chosen wolves are stronger together."

"Are you sure?" I hated to burden them.

"It's part of war." She smiled sadly.

"Part of our group should head back. The rest of us won't be far behind." Aidan nibbled on his bottom lip. "But we have to figure out how to get everyone back in two vehicles."

"We have three." Finn lifted a pair of keys. "I brought the Honda. I can fit four people in it."

Beth leaned back on her heels. "I'm staying back with you two."

"So am I," Endora said, leaving no room to argue. "He saved my life, and I want to help."

"Well, if she's staying back, so am I." Prescott placed a hand on his sister's shoulder even though his attention was on Honor.

"Me too," Samuel said, standing next to Aidan.

With a bigger group staying back, it wouldn't take us long to bury the body so we could get back on the road sooner. "Okay, the rest of you split up between the Honda and the other Suburban, and get home. We should only be an hour later than the rest of you, tops."

"All right." Amethyst hugged April and headed off to the car. "Don't hesitate to call us if you need something."

Caleb headed over to us with two shovels in his hand. It was time to mourn.

AIDAN POURED the last bit of dirt over the grave his brother now lay in. He and Prescott had worked together to dig the grave. Dirt streaked their faces and clothes.

Aidan threw the shovel down, and tears dripped off his chin. *We wasted so much time fighting.*

I wasn't sure what to say to comfort him, but I needed to do something. I pulled him into my arms and let him cry on my shoulder.

So much remorse and regret flowed between us. *He knew how much you cared for him.* Aidan cared about his family. It was why he'd left me. At first, he'd chosen them over me.

A loud sob racked Endora's chest, and she dropped and rocked back and forth. Prescott hurried to her side and wrapped an arm around her shoulders.

The moon rose beyond the trees, indicating it was getting late. I didn't want to rush this, but our time was running out. The longer we stayed here, the more time The Hallowed Guild had to prepare.

"We need to get going," Prescott said softly. "I know it's hard, but there's a lot of shit going on."

"You're right." Aidan pulled away from me and glanced at the grave. "I love you, Bradley. I hope you found peace at last." He took my hand and pulled me toward the coven.

"Come on, sis," Prescott said gently. "Let's get you home."

I glanced behind me, watching Samuel grab the shovels and take up the rear.

As we approached the Suburban, April appeared and held her hand out for the shovels. "I'm sorry for your loss, and we appreciate you standing beside us."

"We're only a phone call away." I hugged her. "They should leave you alone, at least for a little while."

Caleb walked from the house closest to us with a bag on his shoulder. "I'm going with them."

"What?" April's brows furrowed. "Why?"

Aidan looked at me. *Are we going to let him?*

He glanced at Endora with concern and adoration. "I just know I need to go."

It wouldn't hurt to have another witch on our side. Besides, I didn't think we had much of a choice based on what I saw in him.

"Well, I won't force you to stay," April huffed. "But you better be careful and come home soon."

"Yes, ma'am." He grimaced and looked at us. "I mean, if that's okay with you."

"There aren't a lot of options, are there?" Beth snickered, obviously having noticed the same thing as me.

"It's fine," I spoke before anyone else could and headed to the front passenger door.

We all climbed in the car with Prescott, Endora, and Caleb in the very back. The vehicle descended into silence. It'd been a long day and a gruesome evening.

Aidan turned the engine over as I faced the back of the car. "Give us your cell phone." Prescott might have helped us win, but it could be a ruse. We couldn't be too careful.

"Hey," Prescott started but stopped. "Fine." He pulled his phone from his pocket and handed it to Beth. "Here."

"Thank you." Beth broke the phone in half. "There. Now you can't reach out to your father, and he can't track us."

"What the hell?" Prescott growled from the backseat.

"Bite me," Beth retorted. "It's for our own good."

As we hit the main road, a truck swerved on the road behind us, the truck bed flying sideways as their tires squealed. It straightened and sped, even more, trying to catch up with us.

Aidan gunned the Suburban, his hands tight on the steering wheel.

"Can anyone see who's behind us?" I had a feeling I already knew, but I prayed this was just an odd coincidence.

Caleb turned around, and his voice grew frantic. "It's one of those alphas." He pointed at Prescott. "The one you stood behind."

"Shit, it's my dad." Prescott ducked down to avoid being seen.

I glanced around the two-lane road. We were still in an urban area with nowhere to pull over. "We have to shake them."

"Does anyone have a gun?" Beth searched the cup holders like one might magically appear.

"No, Beth, we don't." That would be convenient. Typically, luck wasn't on our side. "But maybe we can look into it if we survive."

"Hey, I'm trying to think on my toes," Beth retorted.

"Are they always like this?" Prescott hunkered, hiding from his dad's sight.

Samuel turned toward the back. "Yeah, but they're worse in life and death experiences."

The thrumming of the truck sounded louder, and suddenly, our car lurched forward, jerking my neck.

"Holy shit. They're going to ram us off the road," Caleb shouted.

We'd gone through hell just to die in a Suburban with a screaming witch.

CHAPTER NINETEEN

The car jarred again, and Aidan held the steering wheel so tightly his knuckles turned white.

We had to figure out a way out of this and fast. The truck was speeding up to hit us again. "Is everyone okay?"

Beth's face looked green. "Define 'okay.'"

A bridge appeared ahead that crossed over a lake. My heart hammered. If we didn't get a handle on our current situation, the truck would shove us over the railing. The moon hid behind some clouds, causing the sky to darken more, and there was no oncoming traffic, thankfully. "Can you use magic to blow out their tire or something?"

We wolves couldn't do anything in this situation, so hopefully, the witches could.

Samuel clapped his hands. "Actually, yeah." A huge grin spread across his face. "Caleb, feel like helping me?"

After a moment's hesitation, Caleb puffed out his chest. "Sure, what do you want to do?"

"Can you control the wind to prevent them from gaining speed? And I'll get a branch or something to pop one of their tires." Samuel lifted his hand, and a whoosh of air hit a tree fifty yards ahead, shaking it so a branch fell.

Caleb spun around in the very back and pushed his hands forward like he was going to stop the car physically. The car slowed as we reached the bridge.

"Dammit, this is harder than I thought." Samuel's arm shook as he brought the limb toward the car, pulling it toward us. Sweat beaded on his forehead. "It's hard to keep up with a moving car."

Aidan gritted his teeth. "We're going ninety, so I'm sure that doesn't help."

"Agh." Samuel jerked his hands to his face, and the branch soared next to the car. He then quickly moved his hands left, and the branch followed. It hit the windshield, cracking it.

The smell of burnt rubber filled the air as the car slammed its brakes and swerved from side to side. It crashed into the bridge's cement railing and came to a grinding stop.

"They're damn lucky they didn't blow through the blockade." Beth let out a breath. "I just knew they were going to wind up in that lake."

"It's because they'd slowed significantly before hitting the side." Aidan pressed the gas even harder. "Someone else might be close behind and ready to take their spot."

We raced over the remainder of the bridge and for the next several miles.

"I think it's safe to slow down." Endora moved closer to Caleb. "They'd be here by now."

"She's right." We all needed to get a handle on ourselves. "Let's slow down some."

Prescott scowled at Caleb and placed his arm along Endora's shoulders, tugging her to him.

"I'm telling you, as soon as I get back, my happy ass is crawling into a comfy bed." Beth yawned. "I've been more tired these past few months than my entire life combined."

"Hell yeah." Samuel wiped his face. "Once my adrenaline crashes, it'll be a struggle to keep my eyes open."

"We still have about an hour and a half to go." It had been a long-ass day, and we still had so much to do. "I have a feeling tomorrow won't be much better." Until this was over, I was pretty sure there were still going to be some days like these. Hopefully, we'd come up with a plan to take on the guild before they attacked another coven.

We all settled in for the next while.

Aidan's pain radiated off him, but had it not been for me knowing him so well and our bond, I wouldn't have had a clue. His eyes were darker, and his body was tense but only marginally. I took his hand. *I love you.*

Only the corner of his mouth tipped upward. *I love you too.*

BACK AT THE COVEN, we found the Honda and other Suburban in Beatrice's parking spot. Aidan pulled in front of the house and turned off the car.

"Wow, this coven is even bigger than the last." Prescott sighed, grabbed the stuff from the very back, and passed it to Samuel.

I headed to the back of the car, looking at the damage. The trunk was completely smashed in. We were lucky Prescott could even get the stuff out.

"Holy shit." Gabby raced from the house, her eyes growing wide. "What the hell happened?"

The others followed and spread apart.

Good. I'd only have to tell the story once. "Some wolves followed us and tried ramming us off the road. Samuel and Caleb did their witchy stuff and saved our asses."

Beth joined me. "She ain't lying."

"Caleb?" Coral scratched her head. "The witch?"

"Yup, the one and only." I found it odd too, but he was clinging to Endora. "Figured it didn't hurt to have another witch in the mix."

"Yeah, we wouldn't have survived without him." Endora marched over and scanned the damage. "It took both of them to derail the car."

"I'm just glad you all got here safe and sound." Beatrice hugged me. "We've been worried sick about you."

"I've gotta say I'm shocked you came back." Rowan rocked on her feet. "I figured you would have run off with your dad."

"In all honesty, I did." Endora's shoulders sagged. "But someone important died for me. That's not something I can overlook, and it was my fault."

Aidan, Samuel, Caleb, and Prescott headed over.

"They told us you picked up another stray wolf and witch." Beatrice held her arms wide. "Welcome to our humble abode."

"Uh ..." Prescott stiffened. "Thanks, I think."

"So, are we all on the same side?" Sage asked and kissed her son on the forehead.

"Yes, I'd say we are." Endora stared at the ground. "I'm sorry I was such a pain."

"You needed time." There was no reason for her to feel bad about that. "We all had to come to terms with death and heartache in our own way. Gabby refused to come with us at first."

"Really?" Endora flicked her gaze up to Gabby. "But you're so dedicated to the cause. How did she get you to join her?"

"She won our fight." Gabby chuckled. "And I've become dedicated along the way. I want to return home without having to worry about a secret society trying to find me or kill my grandmother's coven."

"That does sound nice." Ivory nodded. "To be able to learn about both of our halves without punishment or fear."

Aidan stayed unusually quiet beside me. He was hurting far more than he let on. I glanced at my phone, and it was after midnight. "Let's all get some rest. Tomorrow is a big day."

"How so?" Sunny paused. "Wait ... are we going to try again?"

Yes, we'll try to reveal the pages again. I didn't want to tell Caleb or Prescott too much. I trusted them enough to be here, but not to know all our secrets. *The last thing we need is the book disappearing while we sleep.* "We're going to sleep and start fresh tomorrow. So, yes, let's try it again."

"I don't want to sleep on an air mattress tonight." Logan rubbed the back of his neck. "I'm sore and tired."

Beth rolled her eyes. "Oh, good God, take my room. I can sleep on an air mattress."

"And you two take the spare room." Endora glanced at Remus and Ivory. "You deserve a room to yourself."

"I guess that means all of us get to sleep on the floor." Ada waved us toward the house. "I'm okay with it."

"Rowan, Sage, and I will set a perimeter spell." Beatrice waved the other witches on. "Everyone relax. Tomorrow is a new day."

It took thirty minutes before Aidan and I shut the door to our bedroom. Aidan had helped blow up the four queen mattresses while I'd treated the scratches on Amethyst's face. Her mother would heal them when she returned, but I didn't want to chance them getting infected.

Despite my exhaustion, I needed a shower and to tend to my mate. We would make too much noise out here, so it would be the best place. I took his hand, forcing him to follow me.

His golden eyes glowed. *What are you doing?*

You know what. I turned on the lights and shut the bathroom door. *We haven't had alone time in a while.*

His arousal scented the air. *You don't have to do this.*

I raised an eyebrow. *When have I ever not wanted to do this?* I turned on the water and grabbed towels from the small linen closet. *It's been a long day, and I could use some stress relief.*

He needed to know I loved him and he wasn't alone. The mate bond and sex were the perfect combination.

I sashayed over to him, grabbed the bottom of his shirt, and yanked it over his head. I tossed it aside and placed my hand on the back of his neck, pulling him down to my lips.

He eagerly returned my kiss, and my mind grew hazy. I unbuttoned and unzipped his pants, and pushed them down to the floor.

Dammit, he growled, and his hands fisted in my hair. He pulled back enough to remove my shirt from my body. *You're so damn sexy.* He kissed down my throat and my chest, stopping right at my breasts. In one swoop, he undid my bra and threw it aside. His mouth captured my nipple and bit down gently.

Oh, God. My head leaned back as the sensations flowed through me, warming my body.

You are mine. He groaned as he removed my jeans and panties then hoisted me up against his waist. My legs tangled around him as he headed into the shower.

The soothing water hit my back, and I grabbed the plastic sides of the shower, lowering myself so he slipped inside.

He thrust into me once and paused. *You feel amazing.*

The water helped fuel my need. *Don't stop.* My nails clawed at his back, and I squirmed against him.

His sexy laugh filled my ears. *Patience, little one.* He slammed into me over and over again. My back was against the cold wall, and the water washing over us made our bodies slide even better.

My head became dizzy, and Aidan lowered his lips to my neck, nipping me and bringing me closer to the edge.

I moaned loudly as the orgasm rocked my body, and he jerked as he filled me once more. He stepped back, allowing me to slip off his body, and he kissed me again.

He cupped my cheek. *I'm lucky to have you.*

I'm sorry about today. I didn't want to ruin the moment, but I couldn't escape the idea that it was somehow all my fault. *If I hadn't been marked ...*

Don't you dare. He placed his finger under my chin, forcing my head up. *You are my perfect half, and I would never want you any other way or to be someone else. I'd go to Hell to find you if I had to.*

Hell? I grinned and wrapped my arms around his neck. *What are you saying?*

Stop it. He smiled and kissed me. *You know what I mean. Now, let's get out of the shower before we get yelled at for hogging all the hot water.*

My alarm blared, waking me from a deep sleep. I wanted to press snooze or turn the damn thing off, but there were more important things at stake. I wiggled out of Aidan's hold to grab my cell phone, but he tightened his grip and pulled me back into his chest.

"Turn it off," he grumbled. "I need more cuddle time."

"Did you just say you need more cuddle time?" He was never going to live this down. "I didn't know alpha men said such things. Wait till I tell the others."

"I don't give a damn," he said as he tickled my sides, causing me to squeal. "You're my weakness, and I'm not afraid to admit it."

I jumped to my feet and turned the alarm off. "That doesn't make it any fun, then." Moments like these made me realize we would be okay after everything was done. We had a real relationship to fall back on. "Come on, let's wake everyone up and see what this book has to say."

"All right."

We each threw on jeans and a shirt and walked into the living room. The smell of bacon made my stomach growl. I'd expected everyone else to still be asleep, but they were up and putting away the air mattresses.

I scanned the group. "Where's Sunny, Prescott, and Honor?"

"Prescott and Honor went for a walk together," Beatrice answered as she flipped the bacon over in the frying pan. "And Sunny went to call Eric."

"It's six in the morning." Texas was an hour behind us. "It's five there."

"He texted her and asked her to call him as soon as possible." Amethyst pulled biscuits from the oven. "The others are on their way."

"And I thought I was getting up early." They'd been up for at least thirty minutes before us.

"It's hard to sleep when you want answers." Ada put the last pile of sheets in the closet and turned to me as the rest of our core group came in from the other houses. "It also doesn't help that Beth snores like a bear."

"I do not." She stomped and pouted.

"Don't even lie." Samuel pointed at her. "This has been a common theme for weeks."

"And we've all had to share a room with you." Gabby closed her eyes and cringed. "I can still hear it when it's too silent."

"No, Logan snores as loud as her." Remus lifted a hand. "There's no way in hell it ever gets that silent."

"True story," Aidan said as he sat at the kitchen table.

Sunny linked with our group. *We have a problem. Maverick confirmed the other three packs associated with The Hallowed Guild have almost made it to Mount Juliet.*

No! It's too soon. Barry must have headed straight there once they made it off the bridge.

Honor? We needed to figure out what this book said. *We need you back now.*

Be there in five minutes, she replied.

"The Hallowed Guild packs are converging on Mount Juliet." I began filling in the witches. "We need to get the book and see what the hidden message says."

"It should make it all go away." Sage smiled. "You've won the war. The last piece is just having magic to set everything right. You don't need to worry about The Hallowed Guild any longer."

"Really?" I knew we'd been rushing to get back to Mount Juliet, but could it be that simple?

"That's what we've always believed." Beatrice put the leftovers in the refrigerator and headed into the den. She walked over to the coffee table and pulled out the book. "You now have all six and have proven yourself worthy."

If we hadn't, I wasn't sure what more we could do.

Sunny walked through the front door and over to us. "Are we ready?"

"No, we're waiting on ..." Before I could finish my sentence, Prescott and Honor walked in the back door.

"Everyone's here." Endora stared at the book. "What are we supposed to do?"

Beatrice flipped to the blank pages at the back of the book. "Just like before, each one of the marked girls needs to put their blood willingly on the page. It will then reveal its secrets."

"Are you sure this is safe?" Prescott frowned and stepped closer to Honor.

I didn't have time to even process that right now. "Of course it is."

"So, we'll get our magic?" Endora asked as she looked at the ancient pages.

"That's what we believe, especially after it said we needed to find you to prove the marked girls' worth." Beatrice pulled a dagger from her pocket and handed it to me.

"We'll perform the ritual in the same order we were found." I pricked my finger and dropped my blood onto the page. Then, the girls headed over and followed my lead, ending with Endora.

When Endora's blood hit, the pages flashed, and lights sparked inside them. The blood mixed and swirled then separated. The blood then shot from pages and hit each one of us hard in the chest.

The trapped magic inside me trembled against the cages that held it. The pressure was so hard that I heard the rattling of the walls inside my ears. Then, it popped, and I blacked out.

CHAPTER TWENTY

My head flooded with a mix of magical colors, some I'd never seen before. It was almost iridescent as I walked through a large tunnel. It reminded me of an aquarium where you walked under the water, but instead of liquid, it was a mass of colors that held a strong, addicting buzz.

"I knew you could do it," the original witch said from behind.

Unlike last time, I wasn't surprised. "I had my doubts. I'm just damn glad it's over."

"But it's not." She walked over to me, her blue dress flying behind her and her dark hair pulled into a French twist. "What comes next is the most important."

"Wait ..." That's not what we'd been told. "Beatrice said—"

Endora interrupted me. "They are not the authority." Her features hardened as she took me in. "I forged this, and the next part is what will make you succeed or fail."

"We fought the original alpha's pack." I wasn't above

kicking and screaming like a toddler. "What else could you want?"

"That's why I'm here." She lowered her hand, and a wooden rocking chair magically appeared. "You can now know everything."

"It would've been nice to know all this ahead of time." I stood in front of her and crossed my arms. I wanted all my hostility on display.

She waved her hand to the area behind me. "Sit down."

"Unlike you, I don't have a chair." I pointed at the air behind me.

"You have magic now." Endora lifted a hand. "Think about it, and it'll appear."

"The witches must speak to make spells work." That point caused me great trepidation. How was I supposed to use my magic if I didn't know the spells?

"You aren't like them." She pushed her palm in my direction, and colorful magic similar to what was flowing outside the glass tunnel slammed into me. "I've given you part of my magic."

"But ..."

"No words are needed for you or me. You merely think it, and it'll happen." She crossed her legs and placed her hands on her knees. "Go ahead and try."

I felt silly but didn't want to piss her off even more now that she wanted to share everything. I needed whatever information she wanted to give. I pictured a puffy recliner, wanting comfort.

"See." She laughed and grinned. "A little much but okay."

I turned and found the exact chair I'd imagined. I couldn't believe it had actually worked. I faced Endora again and sat in the chair. "Well, then."

Something like pride filled her face. "You're a natural."

"Will the others have magic like mine?" If there was more to come, they'd need to know how to use their magic as well.

"Similar, but not as strong." She turned her gaze to the lights flashing outside. "Your magic is still growing. Once the colors calm, you'll be ready to awaken again."

"What do you mean 'not as strong'?"

"They will be able to perform magic without sacrifice or words, but your power will be stronger." She shifted in her seat as she settled in. "Your magic is more powerful. If they call fire, they will kindle a forest, but you'll blow the damn thing up. Do you see what I'm saying?"

"Even Endora?" She was descended from her too. "Based on what you said, that we're very distant family, she's a part of you too."

"I couldn't bestow as much magic in her because I had to give her a different gift."

"What kind of gift?" That didn't sound very good.

"She had to lose her mate before she'd cooperate with you." Endora rubbed her hands together. "So ... I had to help fate out by giving her a backup so she wouldn't fall apart completely."

"Caleb?" That was the only person who made sense.

"Yes. He has a small amount of wolf shifter in him, so I was able to create another link." Endora rocked in her chair. "He has a tiny part of the Murphy line in him."

Of course, he did, but my thoughts went to my mate. "Aidan's brother was always meant to die." I hated that Aidan had lost someone he loved.

"It was his redemption." Endora tilted her head. "For him to be willing to sacrifice himself for the woman he loved was beautiful and helped set everything into motion."

"What's next?" It felt like no matter what we did, another challenge hit us.

"Now that you've been awakened, you need to retrieve a relic." She closed her eyes. "Once it's destroyed, the alphas will fall and the true alpha heirs will take their place in the pack, next to their hybrid mates."

"Wait ... is that why we all have alpha heirs as our mates?" This conniving bitch. She'd planned this all and didn't care who she hurt. "Well, one of Endora's mates was the alpha heir."

"Of course. You found the last mate yesterday for the remaining marked girl. This is how you will all help lead the packs and be accepted as an alpha beside their alpha heir. When the other packs see these packs accepting you all as leaders and equals, it will change the entire wolf shifter hierarchy."

She must have meant Prescott was Honor's mate. It made sense with how they'd gone off together this morning. "What kind of relic are you talking about?" I was okay with us being viewed as leaders. We'd all overcome struggles to make us more empathic and approachable.

"It's the original alpha's ring." Endora waved a hand in front of her, and a thick gold ring with a ruby in the center appeared. "It was one of his most beloved treasures, and thus his spirit clings to it and influences the current alphas into thinking exactly like him. With the ring destroyed, the current alphas will perish, but the alpha heirs will be safe since they've never been subjected to his dark soul."

"But Eric, Sunny's mate, is already alpha." Did that mean he was doomed?

"He's newly turned, and he found Sunny within a week of him stepping into that role." Endora lowered her hand, and the ring vanished. "Their bond will save him. She's protecting him from the original alpha, but Murphy is growing impatient, so we need to destroy the ring as soon as possible."

It sounded like we were going on a treasure hunt. "Where can we find it?"

"Where it all began." Endora's eyes darkened. "Mount Juliet, Tennessee."

"What?" For some reason, I hadn't expected that. "Home?"

"Yes. Murphy's ring is handed down to the Murphy pack alpha." She looked upward. "It's almost time for you to go back."

"You're saying I have to remove it from Aidan's dad's hand?" This had to be a dream. "You're joking, right?"

"Oh, don't be dramatic," she huffed. "He knew what he was getting into when he accepted the ring."

"That's comforting," I said sarcastically. "How the hell am I supposed to destroy the ring?"

"The six of you need to use your power at the same time." She stood. "I'll be there to add the extra oomph at the end."

"The Murphy pack is calling all the alphas there." It would be smarter to wait until later when they were gone. "It will be a suicide mission."

"Actually, no." She began to fade. "That's not true. Their witch will locate you and come to you if you don't go there. There's no stopping a battle that has been in the making for centuries."

"So, we need to kill the witch?" How many people would we have to kill?

"No, when you destroy the relic, the witch will turn back to good." Endora appeared as light as a ghost. "The alpha runs a family of witches, and part of the magic protects their souls. She won't perish, but she will hunt you until the ring is shattered."

I had so many damn questions, but the colors were now flowing like a river instead of shooting bursts. As she disappeared, the glass cave began to fracture and crack. No wonder she'd left. I was going to drown.

The glass cracked from one end to the other. There was no use in running. The tunnel went on for as far as I could see.

Seconds later, the colors slowly dripped from the ceiling. Soon, the drips grew larger and larger until the colors poured down and broke the glass even more. The liquid filled the cavern, and I took a deep breath, getting as much air as possible. There was no way I was going to make it out alive.

The colors splashed into me hard, and I fell onto my back as the liquid submerged me. I kicked upward, but there was no point. My vision grew hazy, and my lungs hurt. I kicked and thrashed, but darkness overcame me.

***

Aidan

THE GIRLS DROPPED LIKE FLIES. I barely caught Emma in time before she would have hit her head hard on the ground. The mates rushed to each girl while Prescott went for Honor, Caleb raced to Endora, and Ada reached for Sunny.

"What the hell is going on?" Finn hurried over to Emma, fear clear on his face.

"I don't know." He'd better get his shit together. Emma had my entire focus right now. I laid her down and gently touched her face. "Emma?" The only reason I wasn't freaking the fuck out was because her heartbeat was strong.

"Gabby." Logan's deep voice cracked. "Get your ass up."

"I thought you said they'd get their powers," Beth said desperately. "Not almost die."

"I ..." Beatrice blinked several times, at a loss.

If these girls left us, none of us could survive the heartbreak.

Emma

I SUCKED in a breath and sat upright. Familiar arms held my shoulders, and I turned to see my mate looking broken.

"Oh, thank God." He pulled me against his chest, and tears dropped onto my face. "I was so damn scared."

"I ... I'm sorry." I hadn't meant to scare him, but that hadn't been my call. "Are the others okay?"

"Damn that hurt." Gabby groaned. "It's like I hit the hardwood floor."

"I caught you." Logan sounded both scared and annoyed. "It was nothing like hitting the floor."

I turned in their direction and saw all of the girls coming to. They'd all passed out like I had.

"With those huge-ass muscles, it was exactly like that." Gabby smacked him on the shoulder and rubbed her head. "I feel weird."

It took her saying that for me to realize I did too. The magic was no longer trapped. "It's our powers." I imagined a faint breeze blowing in the room, and within a second, cool air hit my face.

"What the...?" Prescott said and lifted a hand.

Amethyst's face lit up. "You all have your powers."

"Thank God it's over." Sage's body sagged with relief. "This was getting to be too much."

"Is it really over?" Endora leaned against Caleb's chest.

"No." I hated to tell them and kill their spirits, but if we didn't get a plan in place, we would be facing The Hallowed Guild here. "It's not."

Aidan's hands stiffened on my shoulders. "What do you mean?"

"I saw Endora." The words hung heavy in the air, and I stopped the breeze.

"Wait ... I'm right here." Endora stood and looked at me like I was crazy. "Of course you're seeing me again."

"That's also the original witch's name." Everyone's eyes landed on me.

Prescott ran a hand through his hair. "Dad was a son of a bitch for naming her that."

"It doesn't matter." I filled them in.

Once I'd finished, Gabby blew out a breath and said, "Of course, we'd have to fight them at their home base because we haven't had so much other shit to do."

"I don't understand." Caleb took a step back from us. "You had two mates, and I'm one of them. It's still hard to process. What pack am I even from?"

"She said you don't have much shifter in you but enough to form the bond between you two." We didn't have time for a meltdown, but he deserved some answers. "But you're from the Murphy pack."

"And we're mates." Honor grinned at Prescott. "I guess it makes sense."

"You're stuck with me now." He tucked a piece of her hair behind her ear.

"But it'll be over after this, right?" Ivory's eyes met mine.

"It will." I kept my eyes lowered. It was time to tell them the other piece. "But the current alphas will die, and the true alpha heirs will be called to stand in their place."

"Wait ..." Aidan dropped his hands to his side. "I'm going to lose my dad too?"

I'm so sorry. If I could fix it, I'd do it in a heartbeat. I know ...

No ... Aidan took my hand in his. *He's changed. He didn't even want someone to look for Bradley. He's been cold the past few years. It's as if I don't know him anymore.*

"What about Eric?" Sunny's voice held hysteria. "He's an alpha."

"She said he hadn't been the alpha long before you two met." At least, that was some bright news to share. "And that your bond will protect him. He'll be fine."

"But our dads will have to die." Prescott's gaze connected with Aidan's. "It's inevitable."

"Yes, but you don't have to be involved." I didn't want them to blame themselves for their parents' deaths. "But if we don't do this, they'll find us and bring the war here. If we do it here, we won't have a chance to get the relic and end the war."

"It's a no-brainer." Prescott touched Honor's face gently and glanced at his sister. "There is too much at stake to let them win."

"And Logan and Remus." I turned to them. I needed everyone to understand. "You two will be expected to step in for your packs. Our mates were designed to be the new pack alphas with us leading beside you. It's the way to champion in the new hierarchy and make the change across all packs."

"My father treated us like his minions." Remus frowned. "It's not ideal, but I can't stand the possibility of losing Ivory. We all knew this decision would come eventually. We knew it when we were little boys."

"How many people are traveling to Mount Juliet?" I asked Sunny. "Did Eric say?"

"Not too many." Sunny pulled her phone out and scrolled. "He said about five people including the alphas are heading there. They want the strongest of the five to attend."

"They're regrouping and planning to hit here." Aidan stood and paced in circles. "Our pack has a hundred wolves, so with five coming from the other four packs, we're talking about one hundred and twenty."

"We can get most of the coven to join." Beatrice motioned to the door. "We'll round them up now."

"Maybe twenty or so outside our main group here." We didn't need every single one of them there. "The six of us have our magic now."

"But you're untrained," Finn said.

"It doesn't matter." I wiggled my fingers. "Our magic is more like hers. We don't require sacrifices or words. We can control it with our minds."

Coral walked over and bumped my shoulder. "That's incredible."

"Does the book say anything now?" Beth pointed at the book still in Beatrice's hands. "I mean, after all this, there better be something there."

"You're right." Beatrice flipped to the back, and her hands ran over the page. "It's a drawing."

She held it up, and the image of the ring was just as Endora had shown me in the cave. The sides were a thick gold mixed with black, and the ruby was dark and crisp. There was an image of a wolf howling on both sides.

"Dad wears that ring for any special occasion." Aidan sucked in a deep breath. "He had it on during the attack last night."

"I think I have a plan." I pulled out my phone and found my former alpha's number up. "I'll be right back." It was time to see if my family was willing to save my life.

CHAPTER TWENTY-ONE

I walked outside, and my finger hovered over Sam's name. It was time to woman up and speak to the alpha myself, instead of getting Jacob or my parents to do it for me. I needed to do it myself.

Do you want me to join you? Aidan linked, allowing me to choose.

Yes. I would always be stronger with him by my side.

The back door opened, and he stepped outside. *Who are you calling?*

Sam. It was nine in the morning, so he should be up. Not that it mattered. I pressed his name, and the phone rang on the other side.

After four rings, his familiar voice came on the other end of the line. "Hello?"

"Hey." Oh, he didn't have this number, so he probably had no clue who was calling. "It's Emma."

"I recognized your voice." He paused. "Are you okay?"

"Yeah, I am." Starting off by lying didn't bode well for me. "Actually, I'm not."

"Are you hurt?" he asked with concern.

He sounded like he still cared about me. "No, I'm not." We didn't have time to waste. "Have my parents told you everything?" I'd filled them in on the specifics, but I hadn't told them about the dangers we had encountered. They already knew and didn't need me throwing it in their faces.

"They did." He cleared his throat. "You're part witch, and that's why the Murphys hate us."

"It's a little more complicated than that, but that's the gist." Here we went. I took Aidan's hand. I fully expected Sam to say no, especially after what had gone down with Jacob. There was no reason for them to have our backs. "So ... the original alpha who killed the witch, he's influencing his pack, which has splintered into a total of five packs. The alphas from each pack, along with four of their strongest men, are heading or already at the Murphy territory."

"Are you serious?" A door slammed on the other end of the line. "That's why they've been patrolling the territory line."

My stomach dropped, and I put the phone on speaker so Aidan could hear better. "When did that start happening?"

"Two days ago." Birds chirped over the phone line, and I heard Sam's heavy footsteps. "More were gathering this morning."

"They're going to attack." Aidan stiffened. "We need to get there now."

"Shit." Sam sounded scared, and then he was pounding on someone's door. "Josh!" he yelled. A loud bang sounded as if the door had flown against the wall.

He was at my parents' house. "What's going on?"

"Holy shit." I could clearly hear Sam's ragged breathing. "Emma, they got your parents."

"What?" My ears had to be playing tricks on me. They were on their side of the border, following the agreement.

"The men I had patrolling the border aren't responding." Horror laced Sam's words. "They've pretty much declared war. Is that what you were calling to warn me about?"

"No, I was asking if you'd help us fight against them." Anger raged inside me. "But I hadn't even considered this."

"Of course, we'll fight beside you." Sam huffed. "You'll always be part of this pack even if not officially. But we could use your help before we attack. How long until you get here?"

I'll get the others moving. Aidan ran into the house.

"Five hours." It was too long, but there was nothing we could do to change it. "Hold tight until we get there."

"I've already called the pack members together. We'll hold them off until you get here, but hurry up." He hung up the phone.

I rushed into the house, ready to get in the car and roll.

"How many wolves do they have there?" Remus asked and faced me.

"About a hundred, so if our usual group goes, we'll be okay."

"I'm going too." Beatrice grabbed a set of keys and straightened her back.

"Mom, no." Amethyst tried removing the keys from her grasp. "You need to stay here and lead."

"Rowan and Sage will do that." Beatrice arched an eyebrow. "I'm the High Priestess and your mother. You will do as I say."

"Don't be too hard on her." Sage patted Beatrice's shoulder. "She doesn't want her mother to get injured."

"Well, if she doesn't want her mother running into

danger, she shouldn't be either." Rowan faced Amethyst and frowned. "She'll lead when her mother is gone, so she shouldn't be risking her life either."

"Fine." Amethyst's body slumped. "I get it. Let's get going."

Samuel pointed at the set of keys in Beatrice's hand and held two more up. "We've got three Suburbans." He tossed a set to Aidan.

"Honor, Endora, Prescott, and Caleb, ride with me and Aidan." It made sense to keep all the mates together. "Beth, Gabby, Logan, Ivory, and Remus, take the other one. The remaining can ride in the third."

"I'll drive." Samuel threw Beth the other set of keys.

Aidan and I were the first out the door with the others close behind. In minutes, we were pulling out and racing toward home.

FINALLY, around three, we pulled into my parents' driveway. Fortunately, it was long enough for all three cars to fit.

I took in the two-story house I'd grown up in. There was a step-up white porch big enough for two rocking chairs, and the rest of the house was beige siding. Memories of laughter and love played in my head. The white front door was wide open, reminding me that they were in enemy hands.

Footsteps headed my way, and Sam hollered, "Emma!"

It hurt so damn much to look at it. I gladly turned away from my house to face Sam.

He, Jacob, and several other pack men headed our way.

Great, we get to see him right off, Aidan grumbled, but I didn't think he'd meant for me to hear it.

Stop it. I nodded at the alpha and others. *You know I'm all yours, so stop being jealous of the past. We can't change it.*

Fair point. He stood beside me.

"Why am I not surprised that they're with you," Jacob complained as he acknowledged Aidan, Beth, Coral, Amethyst, Samuel, and Finn. He stopped at Prescott. "What the hell are you doing here?"

Shit, I'd forgotten that Prescott had beaten him up. "He's part of my group now."

"Really?" Jacob laughed without humor. "The guy who beat the shit out of me is welcomed into your group with open arms. How fucking convenient."

Sam's forehead was lined with confusion. "Wait ... is this your former roommate?"

"Yeah, the one who beat me to a pulp." Jacob's hand clenched at his side.

"Look, he was trying to protect his sister's secret." That sounded better in my head. "And he's the mate of one of the chosen girls. We have to stick together."

"I'm sorry, man." Prescott grimaced. "It wasn't meant to go down like that. I lost control when she escaped." He pointed at me.

"We don't have time for this shit." Everyone had to see the bigger picture. "He won't hurt you, and the Murphys are going to descend on us at any minute, especially if they figure out we're here."

"She's right." Sam pointed at Prescott and got in his face. "However, one step out of line, and we'll address it immediately."

Prescott breathed heavily but nodded. Under normal circumstances, he wouldn't have allowed anyone to talk to him that way, but ensuring his mate's safety was his priority.

Aidan took my hand and spoke, directing their attention back to the matter at hand, "Are they still patrolling the line?"

"Yes," Harold replied from beside Sam. His hair was graying at the sides, and there were dark circles under his eyes. He was a stout guy, and I hated to see him looking the way he did. He was one of the few pack members who had treated me like family.

"What's the plan?" Beatrice turned toward me, bypassing my former alpha.

Sam's eyes widened at the dismissal, and he opened his mouth to speak.

Beatrice had done that for a reason, so I had to beat him to the punch. "How many shifters are willing to fight?" I turned my gaze on him.

He winced, not liking the fact I'd taken control. "We have at least seventy men here who are willing to fight."

"And we have eighteen here to add to those numbers." We had a strategic advantage. They wouldn't know that the chosen had their powers. "We're outnumbered, but not by much."

Honor rubbed her fingers together. "If we use our magic, it should even the odds, if not land them in our favor."

"Magic?" Jacob's head tilted back. "What are you talking about? Emma doesn't have any magic."

"Yes, I do." He irritated the hell out of me. "It's a recent development."

"Well, maybe if—" he started, but I cut him off.

"My parents have been kidnapped, and I have five packs trying to track us down to kill us." He'd either get his head on straight or I'd cut it off. "So stop being petty, and act like a real alpha heir."

Silence descended upon our group until Sam nodded. "I'm not sure going after them head-on is the right call."

"It's not." Aidan pointed to the right of the border. "There are low trees right over the territory line that go on for several yards." *It's close to where we used to meet.* "We should be able to sneak in there undetected. From that position, it would take about ten minutes to reach the heart of the pack."

"That sounds like a good strategy." Sam rubbed his chin. "We didn't realize how far the branches went on your side of the line."

Jacob pouted. "Dad, you're not seriously listening—"

"Shut it," Sam grunted in the gruff tone he rarely used on his son. "She's right. Protecting our own is more important than your petty jealousy."

"But—"

I cut the idiot off again. "We need to move." I turned to my pack and team. "Hold off using your magic until we have to. The more we can take them by surprise, the more it'll work in our favor."

"Remember, they have a black-magic witch on their side." Aidan cringed. "Now those are worthy of being hated."

"I'll add an amen to that," Prescott said and pointed at Aidan. "That's something we can all agree on."

"Remember, don't kill the witch." I needed to emphasize that. Anyone we could save was worth protecting. "Once ..." I didn't want Jacob knowing more than he had to. "... we finish the job, she can be saved."

"No killing witches." Harold nodded. "Got it."

"Unless it's absolutely necessary for your survival." It's not like we should die for her. "But try not to."

Sam waved for us to follow. "Everyone is meeting at the

tree line."

"Make sure we don't all crowd there." Maybe he wasn't as smart as I'd grown up believing. "We can't alert them to our plan. A scout could spot a group that large."

"Okay." He placed his hands in his pocket. "I'll tell them to stay back and only let a few come through at a time."

"Have two-thirds stay back to swarm the visible line when they catch up with us." Aidan took off toward the spot. "When our group gets through, they'll rush to capture the girls."

"Got it." Sam linked back with his pack. "The small group following us is on the way."

Our group made good time as we approached the section of thick trees with low-hanging branches.

Stay right behind me. Aidan dashed across the open section to the trees and crawled on his hands and knees toward the other side of the border through the small clearing in the branches. *I want to be next to you the entire time.*

I followed after him, respecting his wishes. *Don't worry. I don't want any of us splitting up.*

As we made our way through, small twigs dug into my arms and face. A faint coppery scent alerted me that at least one had cut me and drawn blood.

If anyone ahead of me farts, I'll be pissed, Beth grumbled, following right behind me.

Hell, no, Ada said. *Is that why you rushed to jump ahead of me?*

The more people that are in front of you, the higher the chances are, Beth retorted. *Don't hate me because I thought of it first.*

For you to think about that, do you need to pass gas?

Honor asked with concern. *Because I don't think normal people would think about that unless they had a reason.*

I guess you'll find out. Beth chuckled evilly.

Can we focus? I loved these ladies, but the more stressed they were, the more ridiculous the banter became. *We're going up against a strong pack tied to the original alpha.*

Way to kill the mood. Beth bumped into me. *We were having fun.*

Speak for yourself, Gabby interjected. *You know you can link to each other and not make us all suffer, right?*

We're here, Aidan said sternly. *Now, we need to be serious.* He slowly stood and scanned the area. *No one is around here, so be quiet, and we should be good.*

When he moved aside, I climbed to my feet and moved out of the way of the small clearing. It only took a few minutes for our group to stand on the other side with about fifteen additional men from Sam's pack.

Follow me. Aidan walked quickly toward his home, staying close to the thickest part of the trees. After a few seconds, my heart calmed down from some of the anticipation, but the strong scent of several wolves hit me right in the face. I'd thought we were safe too.

A howl came from the right. I spun around to find five huge wolves not even five feet away, baring their teeth at us.

How is that possible? Ada gasped through our bond. *We should've smelled them.*

The witch reeking of black magic stepped out from behind a tree and waved.

That's how, Beth growled. *Of course, they were expecting us.*

Before I could take a deep breath, a wolf lunged right at me and sank its teeth into my arm. Raw pain darkened the edges of my vision.

CHAPTER TWENTY-TWO

Going on instinct, I nailed the wolf in the nuts. Its jaws loosened around my arm. It whimpered and crumpled to the ground.

Emma! Aidan yelled, but a wolf attacked him before he could help me.

A dull ache rocked through me, but it wasn't the piercing pain like when its teeth had sunk into my skin. *I'm fine. Focus on your fight.* I hated to injure the attacker, but if I didn't, he would strike at me again. I grabbed its head and banged it as hard as I could against the ground.

I turned and found Aidan, Beth, Ada, and Honor fighting the other four wolves.

Where was the witch?

My eyes went back to the tree she'd stood behind, but I couldn't see her. That didn't mean she wasn't around. It was strange, though. Her magic felt gross yet familiar.

The others rushed through the opening, and Beatrice stilled as her hand lifted in the air.

"Is everything okay?" I hoped she wasn't having a heart attack on us or something worse.

"Uh ..." She shook her head and took a deep breath. "Yeah ... I've just never been in a situation quite like this before."

"Yeah, it's something you'll never get used to." And frankly, I'd love to never be in a situation like this again for the rest of my life. Boring was underrated.

The sound of more wolves nagged at me. "They're on their way here like we expected." I spun around to find the other four wolves down for the count. "Is everyone okay?"

"Yes, but you aren't." Aidan rushed over and touched my blood-soaked shirt. "You're already injured, and we aren't five minutes into battle."

"I'll be fine." We needed to focus on the incoming threat. "It's nothing."

"Here, let me heal you." Beatrice placed her hand on my shoulder. "It won't take long."

"You need to reserve your energy." I didn't want her to get tired and wind up hurt. "This is nothing."

"Out of everyone here, you need to be at full capacity." Beatrice's hand turned white as she pushed healing magic into my wound. "Don't pretend you're not the strongest one among us."

I'd purposely left that part out when I'd told everyone about my second encounter with Endora. "How ..." I stopped myself because there were prying ears.

"We can sense the magic in each other." Beatrice dropped her hands to her sides. "I never felt anything as strong as when your power was unleashed."

There was so much I didn't know. I moved my shoulder, and there was only a small twinge of pain. "Thank you." I hated not to show my appreciation.

"Have you reached out to your other pack members?"

Aidan asked Sam as he moved my shirt to examine the wound. "Are they on their way?"

"Yes. They've infiltrated the border." Sam faced his pack. "Everyone shift. I'll stay in human form to communicate with them."

Following his command, the others shifted and were soon on four legs.

We could now hear the wolves breathing, so they'd be here in seconds.

"Wait." Endora hurried to me and stared me in the eye. "I want to be part of the pack."

Sam smiled. "Sure, we'd be ..."

"Not yours." Endora pointed at me. "Hers."

I didn't want her to feel obligated because of the others. "You don't have—"

"Stop it." She held up a hand. "You've been the leader ever since I joined and so damn patient with me. Also, it would be good to be able to communicate with the entire pack." She bowed her head. "You are now my alpha."

Another pack link bond warmed inside me, and moments later, another one connected as well. What the hell? My eyes connected with the source of the second link.

Prescott.

Did you mean to do that? It was a stupid question, but I hadn't expected him to submit to me. Hell, he'd tried to have me killed, though I understood why he'd done it now.

Yes. If my sister trusts you, so do I. He shrugged. *It's not a big deal.*

It sure seemed like it to me, but it was obvious he didn't want to make a big deal about it.

They're here. Logan stepped in front of the group, eager for the fight. *There are at least twenty of them.*

Don't worry, Aidan said with disgust. *More are on their way.*

I need to find that ring. I could use their fighting as a distraction to find the ring. *The longer we wait, the likelier it'll be protected.*

I'm sure Dad has moved it. Aidan turned to Sunny. *Maybe reach out to Eric.*

She pulled her phone out of her pocket and typed out a message. *Hold them off until I get an answer.*

"Let's fight." Sam waved his pack forward, and it was an even match.

Let's head toward the houses. Aidan took my hand and waved the others to follow behind. *We need to find Emma's parents and the ring.*

All of the marked ones stay with me. It felt weird calling ourselves the marked ones. Others had said it with such disdain, but they failed to see that it didn't dictate who we were or what we believed in. Each one of us had a distinct personality. *Once we find the ring, we need to work on smashing it as soon as possible.* By doing that, we'd not only end this war, but my parents would no longer be at risk.

You can't leave the mates behind, Remus interjected. *We're stronger together.*

He was right. We were stronger together.

Eric just texted back. He'll meet us at the edge of the housing, Sunny said happily. *He has the ring.*

What? I hadn't expected it to be easy.

Yeah, I'm shocked too. Sunny had a huge smile on her face. *But we'd better go.*

Is it normal for someone to be that happy right now? Prescott sounded unimpressed. *I mean, we're fighting.*

She's about to see her mate, Honor replied patiently. *She hasn't seen him in a while.*

Let's go meet up with him. I didn't want to alarm Sunny, but getting to him was a priority before something happened. *And end this thing once and for all.* I faced Sam. "You guys stay here and fight. We're going to find the alpha and my parents."

"The others are almost here." Sam glanced over his shoulder at me. "We should be good."

"Stay quiet and close." I glanced at the witches that we wouldn't be able to communicate with soon.

"We'll take the back," Logan said and pointed at Remus. "That way, we can let you know if something is about to happen."

"Sounds good." I looked for any sign of the witch, but nothing popped out. Hopefully, she'd run away even though it was highly unlikely.

"Everyone be careful." An unsettling feeling ran down my spine. "The witch could be hiding in plain sight, and we wouldn't know."

"The air around her should be distorted." Amethyst lifted her hands from her sides. "It will be faint, but with your wolf eyes, you should be able to see it."

"Good to know." Prescott took Honor's hand. "Stay close to me."

I tried to keep a level head, but it was hard. *We need to find my parents before it's too late.*

Aidan took off at a steady pace, and our group followed behind. Amethyst and Beatrice stayed close to me as they cautiously watched for anything alarming.

The trees were thinning, which meant we were getting close to their living quarters. The sound of water rippling across a pond hit my ears right before it came into view on our right. Fish jumped up, trying to catch whatever skimmed the surface.

It'd have been nice not to have any cares in the world.

We're close. Aidan linked with the entire pack. *Dad's house is right in the middle. He wanted to ensure we were the most protected home in the entire neighborhood.*

As alpha, he should have accepted the same risk as his people. He was a special kind of asshole to put himself ahead of those he was meant to protect. Somehow, I bit my tongue despite knowing Aidan would agree.

Huge-ass houses were now ahead. I'd thought Barry's pack had expensive houses, but this was over the top. The houses had to be in the upper-middle-class range with brownstone fronts, large curvy driveways, and at least two stories.

Holy shit. Beth wasn't one to not speak her mind. *Are you rich or something?*

No, the houses are hundreds of years old. Everyone could feel Aidan's frustration. *It requires a lot of upkeep, but Dad demands that we don't rebuild.*

The closer we got, the more aged the homes looked. However, they were sturdy and nice. The smell of wolf slammed into me, and a branch cracked only a few feet away.

I spun around and found Eric stepping out from behind a tree.

Sunny's face lit up as she took a few steps in his direction. "Oh, thank God."

"Don't," Eric said briskly.

Hurt flashed on her face before I saw the air surrounding him.

"The black magic witch is behind him." Or I thought she was behind him. "Sunny, get back."

The witch appeared with a scowl. "Now, that wasn't fun." Her gaze landed squarely on Beatrice and then Finn.

"Sorry if we ruined your good time." If she was here with Eric, that meant the alphas had to know he helped us.

"No, I'm still having fun." She smirked and snapped her fingers, though she frowned slightly.

Barry, Maverick, and two other wolf shifters appeared out of thin air. They were spread out and circling us.

One looked like an older version of Remus with those same striking green eyes, but his hair had gray peppered throughout. The other alpha appeared cruel. There was no other way to explain it. He had to be in his mid-thirties, but I could feel the darkness in him. In some ways, the darkness poured more from him than the witch.

"My son, you should've known better than to come here." Maverick tsked. "But I should've known you'd lost all your senses when you chose a fucking bitch over your family."

A vein in Aidan's neck bulged. "Do not talk to her that way."

"Or what?" Maverick chuckled evilly. "Do you think you can actually win?"

"Not with that piece of shit on your team." The cruel guy stepped toward Logan. "Or do I need to remind you what's at stake?"

That was the sicko who had killed his father and taken his sister as his mate. My stomach turned in disgust. "You can burn in Hell."

The asshole glanced at me, and his brow furrowed. "Why do you even care?"

"Because unlike you, he's my pack and family." These packs cared about dominance and nothing else. "Which makes his sister our family too."

Something softened on Logan's face, and his gaze met mine. *You really mean that.*

Of course, I do. We would protect each other and anyone we cared about. *When you're alpha, you'll make things right.* It became clearer with each step how messed up these guys were.

"I still can't get over it." Remus's dad stared right at his son. "You left your family for this?"

"Ivory is my fated mate." Remus lifted his chin. "And she's good. There's no way she deserves to die."

"See, that's what they do to them." Barry waved his hand toward our group. "Use their witchy wiles to seduce our sons."

"Yes, that's exactly what we did," Honor said sarcastically as fuck. "We shook our magical breasts in their faces to render them senseless."

"For Christ's sake." Beth sighed. "She might be my new shero."

"Don't forget, *Daddy,*" Endora said, emphasizing the last word. "You're the one who tried to have a marked daughter and kept me by your side."

"You did what?" Maverick's arrogant demeanor slipped. "She's your daughter?"

"Oops." Endora placed a hand over her mouth. "I forgot. It's a secret."

Barry glared at her. "I kept her as leverage in case the curse came to fruition."

The tension hung thick around them. "How's that leverage working out for ya?" We needed to get them upset so they didn't focus on us.

"And what's your excuse?" Maverick turned his attention to Eric. "You're a fucking alpha."

"Maybe we've been wrong this entire time." Eric clutched the ring. "Have you ever considered that the original alpha was wrong?"

"How dare you say such a thing?" Maverick spat, and his nostrils flared. "If your dad could hear you, he'd turn over in his grave."

"What have we ever done to you?" Beatrice asked.

"You live." Maverick's eyes landed on her, and he grimaced. "You pull from nature, which isn't natural. No one should be able to bend nature to their will. To manipulate their surroundings and be led by women. Everything you stand for is wretched."

"Yet, you have a black magic witch working for you." Finn stepped in front of Beatrice, shielding her from the alpha's sight. "How does that make any sense?"

"It's a necessary evil." Maverick motioned to the witch. "We need her to set things right."

"You mean to kill us." Gabby wrinkled her nose in disgust. "And she's willing, so you're all meant for one another."

I wanted to ask about my parents, but it might put me at a disadvantage. "Is that what you're going to do? Kill us?"

"And your parents." Maverick smiled so wide that his yellow teeth peeked through. "Let's not forget them."

Don't overreact. Aidan touched my arm. *He wants you to have a meltdown.*

I'd never give him the satisfaction. Even if I wanted to break down. If I wanted to save my parents, I had to keep a level head. "Of course, I haven't."

Eric caught my attention and flicked his eyes down to his hand.

Everybody get ready. He was about to make a move, but I wasn't sure what. *Something is about to happen.*

Eric lifted his arm and threw the ring right at us. I reached out to catch it, but a strong gust of wind swirled around us.

A loud, evil laugh filled the air, and our group rose eight feet off the ground. The dark witch held up her hand, which now contained the ring. "Looking for this?"

"It's time for war." Maverick focused on me. "I've been waiting to kill you since the day you were born."

The wind stopped, and then we fell.

CHAPTER TWENTY-THREE

I closed my eyes and pictured the breeze underneath us. I wasn't sure if I had to picture it, but I wasn't taking any chances.

We'd only fallen two feet before my powers kicked in.

"Make them fall," Maverick demanded.

"I ..." The dark witch blinked. "... did."

"What the...?" Beth flapped her arms erratically like they were keeping her in the air. "How is this possible?"

I glanced down at the air circling us. We were still high off the ground. The drop could easily harm the witches. *Shut it.* I was hoping they'd think it was one of the full-blooded witches keeping us upward.

"None of them should be strong enough," the witch stuttered.

"Remember, I'm getting older." Beatrice straightened her shoulders at the witch. "Which means I'm in better control of my powers." An edge laced her words. "Things aren't always as they seem, are they?"

The dark witch grimaced.

Something odd transpired between the two of them, but

I'd have to figure it out later. I asked the wind to lower us slowly, and it answered my request.

Damn, she's stronger than I realized, Ada said in awe. *I never knew.*

It was me. I wouldn't lie to them. *Beatrice is covering for us. We need to keep our powers secret for as long as possible. Marked ones, just ask nature to do your bidding, and it'll respond.*

The alpha of Logan's pack pulled out a knife and threw it, aiming for Logan's heart.

Not happening. Gabby lifted a hand, and the dagger bounced off an invisible wall.

"No more fooling around." Maverick pointed at me. "This ends now."

Since we were only a foot off the ground, I released the wind, and we fell to our feet.

Howls sounded outside as the alphas called their wolves to them. Things were about to get worse.

Aidan rushed his dad, and I made my way to the witch. I needed that ring. The fight needed to end before it truly began.

"I'd be careful if I were you." The witch's arrogance fell right back into place. "You don't know how to fight magic."

I steadied my focus and called for the wind. Maybe she'd like a taste of her own medicine.

The wind picked up and circled around her. Her dark braids lifted in the breeze, and a sinister smirk filled her face. "Somebody has been hiding their abilities."

I pushed my hand forward, and the wind knocked her to her knees. I then made the force bend her body to the dirt. I glanced over my shoulder to check on Aidan, who battled with his father. He was holding his own.

"You won't get away with this," the witch said through

gritted teeth. "There is no way you can come out of this unscathed."

"Do you think I'm stupid enough to listen to your threats?" I strolled over and casually squatted next to her. "You don't scare me."

"But I should." She hissed, "Fulgur venire." Static charged around us. "You should never underestimate someone who's lost everything."

My hair stood on end, and that's when it clicked. I jumped away moments before a huge lightning bolt struck where I'd just been standing. My hold on the wind vanished. It was a damn good thing Endora had told me not to kill her because that was exactly what I wanted to do.

"You bitch." I doubted she could ever gain redemption. "I'm not feeling much love for you right now."

She stood again. "Same." Then, her voice lowered. "Adducam interitum tempestate."

Dark storm clouds rolled in faster than I'd ever seen anything before. "What's the point of all this?" She had to have something at stake.

"I lost everything." She stepped toward me. "And now, you will too."

Fifty wolves ran into the clearing, attacking our group of eighteen. I had no way to connect with Sam and ask for backup. We were at their mercy.

Everyone, use your magic. There was no time to hide what we could do. If we did, we'd die. There was no alternative. *Hit hard and fast. We have to take them by surprise.*

Those few seconds of distraction were all the witch had needed before she disappeared with the ring still in her possession.

Fuck! I wanted to yell, but there was no point in using

my energy like that. I needed to channel it toward these assholes.

I spun around and checked on everyone. The wolves were literally descending, causing hell on earth.

Aidan still fought his father as four ran over to gang up on him.

Rain fell around us, courtesy of the witch.

Might as well use it to my advantage. I called for the rain to collect and pushed a huge burst of water at the wolves. They flew in the air and landed hard on their backs.

Before they could move, I called vines out of the earth and wrapped them around the wolf shifters.

Hell yeah. Honor linked to me. *Great idea.*

At least I'd inspired them. I turned to find a wolf running right at me, throwing caution to the wind. I looked up as lightning came barreling out of the sky. I rolled out of the way right as it crashed beside me. The impact jarred me, and I fell on my ass.

Emma! Aidan cried through the bond. *Are you okay?*

Yeah, I'm fine. Other than my ass throbbing and the wolf now only a few feet away. *Focus on your own fight.* I needed him to stay safe.

I didn't want to kill any of these wolves, which was so damn problematic. When our mates took over the packs, they'd be dealt with and forced to accept the new way of life. Their deaths would be pointless and only needed for survival.

The most effective way of handling them was with the vines. Once they were locked in place, I didn't have to focus any more magic on them. The wolf leaped, and I called the vines, catching him in mid-air. They wrapped around his torso and yanked him to the ground. He landed with a huge thud, and they wrapped around his four legs.

Claws dug into my back moments before teeth sank into the back of my neck. Pain ripped through my body. I'd been so focused on the wolf attacking from the front that I hadn't paid attention to my back.

I reached over my shoulder and sank my fingers into its eyes. Not as deep as that one time but enough for its hold to loosen and him to whimper. I then carefully slipped my hand into its mouth and rammed my fingers back. It gagged and released its hold.

Aidan slammed into the wolf and reached down, breaking its neck. *You're injured.* He came over to me and touched my neck. Blood poured from the wound.

It's fine. Where's your father?

I don't know. He sighed. *He took off when I came over to you.*

Maverick had to be meeting up with the witch. *In what direction?*

Toward the houses. Aidan dropped his hand, his face lined with worry. *You're bleeding a lot.*

I'll be fine. My shifter abilities would heal me in no time. *We need to follow him.* I glanced around, and we were handling the wolves fine. Over half of the shifters were tied up with vines, and the alphas were busy focusing on their sons. I linked with everyone, needing the others to come with me. *We need to find the ring.*

We can't leave. A wolf charged at Remus. Ivory raised her hands and sent it flying across the clearing. It slammed into a tree. Vines snaked around the wolf, suspending him.

More wolves ran into the clearing with Sam leading them on.

Thank God, backup had arrived. *That's Sam. They'll take over the fighting. We need to go if we want this to be over.* I ran over to the group and pointed at Caleb, who was actually holding his own. "Come with us." I was being bossy, but I needed the mates of all the girls with us or they wouldn't be able to concentrate.

Sunny shook her head, and she fought by her mate's side. *I can't leave Eric.*

I figured. Get him to come too. A wolf tried sneaking up behind me, and I turned, blowing him across the clearing.

When I faced the group again, all of the marked girls and their mates headed my way. I hurried over to Beatrice. "Can you help Sam fight? We're going after the ring."

"Be careful." Beatrice took my hand. "And call us if you need us."

"We don't have a link." It was an odd thing to say. "So ..."

"You have nature on your side." Beatrice patted my arm. "Be creative." She turned away and muttered, "*Deflo.*" The wolf closest to her flew back several feet.

"Wait ... I just understood what you said." I didn't have time for this, but I was still reeling. "How is that possible?"

"Because you've unleashed your magic." She kept her focus on the pack. "You are allowed to hear it now."

Emma, come on. Aidan linked with me. *We need to hurry. I bet he's with your parents.*

"Let us know if you need anything." If I could get creative, so could she.

Our group followed Aidan through the neighborhood. Occasionally, we would pass by a house with women and kids looking out.

I couldn't believe that the alpha would jeopardize their safety by running back to his place.

Here it is. Aidan motioned to a house that looked the same as the others but slightly bigger. *If I know him, they'll be down in the basement.* He ran to the side of the house and pointed to a staircase that led down to a cement basement.

Of course, there would be a basement. *Everyone be careful.* The rain stopped, and my blood ran cold. Apparently, Maverick and the witch knew we were here.

Aidan and I led the group down the stairs, and when we turned the corner, I found my parents each bound to a chair, their backs touching. Blood soaked my father's shirt around his stomach, and my mom's greasy brown hair hung limp against her face. They were both unconscious.

"It's about time you showed up." The dark witch stood against the back wall, grinning until Finn joined us. "Why is the witch here?"

"Does it matter?" That was strange. Why would Finn's presence bother her? "Let my parents go."

"With pleasure." Maverick stepped from the back of the room, the ruby ring on his hand. "There's only one catch."

"No," Aidan growled. "No way."

"What's the catch?" I had a feeling I already knew.

"Them for you." Maverick turned the ring on his hand. "It's actually a real bargain."

"I said no!" Aidan bellowed, his wolf bleeding through.

We should do it now. Gabby linked with us all. *They won't expect it.*

"I wasn't talking to you, boy." Maverick tensed. "I was done talking to you when you took her side."

Logan rushed at Maverick, but the witch said, "*Ignis.*"

His shoes caught on fire, and chaos ensued.

In seconds, Maverick lifted Logan by his neck, and Gabby ran over to them.

I called for water, and it appeared from the air and drenched his shoes, extinguishing the flames.

I had to get Logan out of Maverick's hold before we did anything. I didn't want Logan to get hurt in the crossfire.

The ground vibrated as I made the Earth tremor. I focused it all under Maverick, making his body rattle. I'd have it swallow the asshole whole if needed, but we had to get the ring first.

"What the hell is going on?" Maverick's eyes locked with mine. "You're doing this aren't you."

"Yes." I wanted him to know it was me. I needed him to think I was willing to risk it all. "Give us the ring or we'll all suffer the consequences."

"You don't have it in you," he said, but terror filled his eyes.

I dug into my magic even more. The ground shook so hard that my teeth clacked together. I supported the walls with my magic, but he didn't know that. I wouldn't allow us all to die.

Maverick fell to the ground as the floor underneath him cracked, releasing Logan from his hold.

The alpha turned to the dark witch. "Do something!"

"Don't." I glared at the witch. "This isn't half of what I can do." I kept my hold on the ground and directed fire right at the witch's feet as she began chanting.

"Agh." She stopped and began stomping her feet, trying to get the fire extinguished. "That's not possible. You can't do two spells at the same time."

Encouraged by her disbelief, I added a third element to preoccupy her. I lifted her into the air preventing her from trying to extinguish the flames.

Now that both of them were busy, there was no time like the present. I stopped all the chaos and dropped the dark witch to the ground and focused on our end goal. That was the only way to end this.

There's no time to waste. I'd thought we needed to get the ring from him, but why? We could destroy it on his hand. *Channel all your magic into the ring.*

On it, Honor chimed in.

Gabby stopped, and her eyes locked on the piece of jewelry.

Our magic charged the air as we worked together.

"No. What are you doing?" The dark witch called out. "De—"

Before she could finish the words, Aidan and Remus were upon her. Remus wrapped his arm around her neck, choking her, and Aidan punched her in the face, knocking her unconscious.

She dropped to the floor as Caleb and Finn ran over to help Logan.

"No ..." Maverick's eyes widened. "You have to surrender."

There was no way in hell we were doing that. *Push harder.*

Maverick rushed me, but Eric blocked his advance. I pushed even more of my energy into the ring. The edges of my vision darkened, and the ring began to sizzle.

"Ow." Maverick jerked back and waved his hand. "What are you doing?"

Harder. We were finally making progress, but I wasn't sure how much more I could handle. My head was growing dizzy, and I felt like I might pass out.

The ring sparked, followed by a hiss.

I don't know ... I didn't let up, but my body sagged. *How much longer ...*

Something flickered out of the corner of my eye, and the original Endora appeared right before me. A proud smile filled her face, and she touched my shoulder.

The crazy thing was that no one else seemed to see her. I had to be delusional.

Her warm hand touched my skin. "You've done well and righted the wrongs of the past." Her body faded, and sparkles took its place. "Endora and Caleb are meant to watch over the witches, and the five of you are to rule the packs by your mates' side and ensure all shifters and witches are treated as equals."

It made sense, but I had so many questions. Before I could ask anything, she disappeared. The sparkles were thick and multi-colored. My eyes closed of their own accord, and magic slammed into me. It pushed toward my center and mixed with my magic.

Unadulterated power flowed through my veins and nourished my body. Now that I could function again, I channeled my new magic into the ring.

"No." Maverick tried to yank the ring off his finger, but it was too late. The metal turned runny, and the ruby flickered from view.

I had a feeling we had to give it our all. *Use every ounce of your magic.*

I'm about to faint! Sunny cried through the bond. *I don't know how much longer I can last.*

Me too, Ivory said.

I groaned as I channeled everything inside me.

"Stop!" Maverick cried. "Please."

But it didn't matter. Right when we were all about to give out, the runny metal congealed then shattered into millions of small pieces.

"Nooo!" Maverick screamed and crumpled to the floor. His body began to shrivel.

Get back! Aidan yelled. *All of you, get back.*

The girls and I stumbled backward as the alpha's body turned to dust.

Was it finally over?

Aidan, Logan, Remus, and Prescott groaned as they all collapsed.

What's wrong? I rushed to Aidan and pulled him into my arms. *Are you hurt?*

If I'd done all this just to lose him anyway, I wasn't sure I could survive. His breathing was ragged. *Aidan.*

I'm fine. Aidan's eyes slowly opened, the gold glow bright. *Dad's bond transferred to me. I can feel the pack in my chest.*

Now that he mentioned it, I felt hundreds of new, warm alpha connections pop up inside me. *I can feel it too.*

Aidan stood, and I turned around to find the other alpha heirs sitting up.

You're all alphas now, aren't you? The madness was finally over.

We are. Prescott laughed and pulled Honor and Endora in for a hug.

But it wasn't time to celebrate yet.

CHAPTER TWENTY-FOUR

I rushed over to my parents and cringed. Their hands were bound together, and the rope dug into their skin, making their wrists raw, leaving blood to drip on the floor. "Dammit." It enraged me that they were hurt because of me.

"Here." Finn bent next to me and pulled out his knife. "This will be faster." He slowly cut through the ropes, making sure the sharp edge didn't nick their skin.

In seconds, the rope fell off.

"Uh ..." Mom moaned as her head moved to the side.

I grabbed her shoulders, holding her steady. "Hey, you're okay."

"Emma?" Her words ran together. "Iz ... that ... you?"

"Yes, I'm right here." I pushed her hair off her face. "You're safe now."

"Here, I can get this side," Eric said as he ran over to the other side. "Someone needs to grab him so he doesn't fall out of the chair."

"Got it." Sunny stood over my dad and touched his shoulders. "Let's get them out of here."

How's everything going over there? I linked with Aidan, who had walked back over to the witch.

Uh ... He hesitated for a second. *Her skin is melting off.*

What? That made no sense whatsoever. Why had Endora asked us to protect her if she was going to die anyway? *Is she breathing?*

Yeah ... he said with disgust. *But damn. Are your parents okay?*

They will be. They hadn't been tortured too badly, so there was that. *But I need to get them home.*

Mom fell forward into my chest, and Dad did the same to Sunny.

"Hey." I lowered my face to hers. "Can you stand?"

"I think so." She placed her hands on my shoulders, and I tried to ignore the blood that coated my shirt. "Once I get to my feet, I should be fine." She stood on shaky legs and fell forward, her arms wrapping around my neck.

Pain exploded down my spine and into my head. I tried not to jerk back, but a loud cry left me.

"What's ..." Mom started, but Aidan rushed to me. He pulled Mom away from me and steadied her against his chest.

"Are you hurt?" Mom's face was lined with concern. "Did I cause it?"

"No, it's fine." I didn't want to worry her. "It'll heal in a day or two."

"A day or two?" she asked loudly.

"Emma, we need help with your dad." Sunny lifted him gently off her. "He's not rousing."

"Josh!" Mom cried. "The witch burned him when she was trying to get him to spill where you were."

I hurried over to him and asked for nature to splash cold water in his face. As soon as I had the thought, it happened.

"Ugh." He groaned, and his hands went straight for his stomach. His body tensed, and he shoved Sunny in the chest hard. She stumbled back.

"Hey!" Eric barked. "Don't hurt her."

"Calm down." I touched Dad's arm. "You're safe, Dad. It's just us."

"What?" He blinked and turned in my direction. "Emma, you have to get out of here. They're ..." He stopped as he took in the room.

"It's over." At least, I hoped it was. We still needed to get back to the clearing. "You and Mom are safe now."

"I thought ..." He wrapped his arms around me and winced, but he still hugged me tightly. "Oh ... thank God."

My eyes teared up from the agony of the bite wound.

"Josh, stop." Mom stumbled over and smacked his hand. "She's hurt."

Dad dropped his arms. "Oh, are you—"

"I'm fine." They had to get out of here before I lost patience with them. "Can you stand?"

Mom rubbed her wrists. "I can walk now."

"As moving as this is, we still have a lot to do." Gabby pointed her thumb at the door. "There's still a lot going on."

"What does that mean?" Mom asked, her dark green eyes full of worry. "Is something wrong?"

"There's a huge fight going on out there." Endora took her mate's hand. "But hopefully, it'll be over soon."

"Wait ..." Dad turned to face Aidan. "You let my daughter get hurt."

"No, he didn't." My dad was nothing like this pack, but he also couldn't grasp women being true alphas either. "He was fighting, and I lost focus on my surroundings."

"That's the—"

"Dad," I growled. "I'm just as capable of fighting as he is."

"Even more so." Beth lifted her fingers and wiggled. "She's got those magic fingers."

My stomach sank. Sam's pack could still be in danger. "Did you call the packs down? We need them to stop fighting if they haven't already."

"Shit, I hadn't even thought about doing that." Remus sucked in air. "But you're right."

"My pack wasn't fighting." Eric looked up. "They were told to stand in the woods and wait until they heard from me."

I've commanded them. Aidan squeezed my hands. *But we still need to get out there. They grew up hating witches.*

"Oh, my God." Finn hurried over to the witch that Logan was still hovering over.

"What's wrong?" Ada asked. "Is she okay?"

"Yeah, but it's ..." Finn lowered his voice. "... my mother."

Logan glanced from Finn to the woman. "How is that possible?"

"Because the alpha captured me and coerced me to do things for him." A faint voice answered, and the witch sat upright. She wiped the thick liquid off her skin, revealing warm, natural-looking skin. "He made me do things that turned me dark."

It was a miracle that his mother had survived and was standing right before us.

"Why did you do anything for them?" Finn asked, stepping away from Wanda.

"They used your father as leverage." A sob racked her body as she held herself. "And after I turned dark, they killed him in front of me. I lost my humanity."

"Are you okay?" I understood why Finn needed space. Not only had he grown up thinking his parents were dead, but now he'd learned that his mother was a witch performing black magic. That wasn't easy to digest. "If so, we need to get back to Beatrice and the others."

"Yeah, I'll be fine." She stood and reached out to her son. "Finn ..."

"No, not right now." Finn turned his back to his mother and headed to the steps.

Ada bit her lip and ran after him.

Wanda's now amber eyes landed on me. "I've lost him, haven't I?"

"No. Family is important to him." I patted her shoulder, trying to ignore the ick on her. She needed comfort right now. "But he thought he lost you, so he's in shock. Just give him time."

"What is that all over you?" Beth's nose wrinkled. "It doesn't smell, but it's gross."

"It's the black magic leaving my body." She lifted her arms and looked down. "It clogs your pores and changes you from the inside out."

Beth scratched her face. "So, kind of like zits?"

"You're so eloquent." Gabby snorted and rolled her eyes.

I waved to the group. "We should hurry." My attention fell back on my parents. "Can you make it?"

"We'll be fine." Dad shuffled his feet to the door. "I've already started healing."

Aidan stood next to me, and within minutes, we were back in the clearing where we'd left the witches and wolves fighting.

They were all standing around, looking confused.

"Are you okay?" I made my way to the witches and

glanced at each witch. They all seemed okay with no visible injuries. Finn stood there scowling, with Ada right beside him.

"Yeah, we are." Beatrice ran a hand over her face. "You destroyed the ring right when we were about to lose." Her eyes then landed on Finn's mom. She ran over to her and took the oozy witch into her arms. "Wanda? I thought that was you."

"I'm so ..." Wanda sniffled. "... sorry."

"There's nothing to be sorry for."

The pack is giving me a hard time. Aidan linked with the group. *They want to continue fighting.*

Eric linked in. *My pack does too.*

Wait, how are you linked with me? He hadn't submitted.

Aidan is the main alpha over all five packs, and he sees you as his alpha. Eric nodded at me. *So we're connected now.*

That was unexpected. *We can't allow their hatred to continue.* It was strange because I thought I'd be able to mind link with all five packs since Aidan was part of my pack, but I couldn't. *We need them to shift back into human form so we can talk.*

We'll tell them, Remus confirmed.

After a few seconds, Aidan connected with us again. *They're heading back to change.*

Let's get the witches out of here. It might help things. I headed over to Sam and pointed at the coven. "Do you mind heading back and letting them go with you?"

The wolf nodded and turned. His pack followed behind him.

"Go with them." I faced the witches and my parents. "We'll be back there soon."

"Are you sure?" Mom asked. "I can stay."

"No. Go back and let the witches help tend to you." I squeezed her arm gently. "I'll be there soon, promise."

"I'm staying here with you and the other wolves." Finn lifted his chin, ready to fight me. "I don't want to leave Ada."

"That's fine." He wanted space, and this was his chance to process everything a little longer.

The other wolves headed back to the houses, listening to their alphas. Now was the time for change to begin.

AIDAN, Remus, Logan, Eric, Prescott, Finn, Caleb, Ada, Beth, and I, along with the other mates, waited outside of Maverick's house—wait, it was actually Aidan's and my house—for the pack members to show.

Did you call for even the women and children to come? There would be no better time to begin treating them as equals. *We need to talk to everyone.*

Yes, I made sure to include everyone. Aidan took my hand, rubbing his thumb along the side. *It'll be okay. They will accept you; I'll make sure of it.*

That was part of my concern, but not the only thing. *I need them not only to respect me but the other women in the packs as well.*

Don't worry. Beth bumped her shoulder into mine. *We'll make sure of it.*

We? I loved that she was all-in with us. I didn't know what I would've done without her beside me this entire time. She'd been my rock long before Aidan was. *Is there a mouse in your pocket?*

Oh, dear God! Gabby complained. *That's something an older person would say.*

I can't help that I'm an old soul. It was oddly comforting that we were all going back and forth. It made it feel real and that maybe things were finally working out. *Don't hate.*

I think it's cute, Ivory said.

Guys, they're heading this way, Sunny interrupted.

I stiffened as I saw the hundred or so members of Aidan's pack making their way here from their homes and the sixteen members of the four other packs stepping out from our home.

It was still strange to think of this place as our home, but I knew that was our destiny. The twelve of us would lead the packs and ensure peace among wolves and witches.

The sixteen other wolves walked over and joined the main pack.

Aidan stepped forward, addressing everyone. "Today, we mourn the loss of our alphas and celebrate the start of a new era."

"What kind of new future?" a tall, muscular shifter asked. "One where we avenge the deaths of our leaders and kill all the witches?"

The group cheered.

"No. One where we live in peace with our own kind and the covens." Aidan's jaw clenched as he stood in front.

"That's stupid!" the tall, scary one from Eric's pack shouted. "Tell 'em, Eric."

"I agree with him." Eric took Sunny's hand. "And my mate will be leading by my side."

"A woman?" another yelled from the back. "You can't be serious."

"Aren't they the marked ones?" The man from Eric's pack jabbed his finger in Sunny's direction. "You cut her throat and killed her. I saw you."

"Then, she's back from the dead!" another person yelled. "That's what witches do."

"That's enough." This wouldn't be tolerated. "It doesn't matter if we're marked or not; we are wolf shifters as well."

"See, that's what ..." someone else shouted, but I couldn't tell who. That was how damn angry I was getting.

Alpha will laced my voice. "As my mate said, this is a new beginning." I stepped forward, standing shoulder to shoulder with him. "In this pack, women will be treated as equals, and covens will be allies."

"But ..." The tall man closest to me tried to speak, but I glared at him, shutting him up. He stood and ran at me.

Aidan's body coiled, ready to react, but before he could, I stilled the air around the man, freezing him in his tracks.

Figures. Aidan chuckled through our bond. *You're amazing. Have I told you that?*

Not today, I quipped back as I stepped up to the frozen man. "You will not threaten any of my kind, especially in my presence." I lifted my head just so I could look down my nose at him. "Do you understand?"

"Yesss," he replied the best he could since his mouth couldn't move.

"You bitch!" someone hollered behind me.

"Emma, watch out!" Aidan screamed as a strong gust of wind blew behind me.

"Do not hurt her." Endora's words were low and clear. "Like she said, you will not hurt any of our kind."

I released my hold on the frozen guy, and he stumbled to the ground. I linked to Endora. *Thank you.*

You're my sister. Her words were full of love. *Of course, I'd protect you.*

It's crazy how much our relationship had evolved. I turned back around and addressed the shifters. "If you have a problem with this new order, you are more than welcome to leave. Unlike the prior alphas, we will not force you to stay." I paused, eyeing the entire group. "However, if we hear of anyone causing issues, we will intervene."

We had to be strict and hold firm.

"And do all the alphas agree to that?" a girl only a few years younger than me asked.

Remus nodded. "We do."

"As do I." Logan's white eyes glowed, ready for someone to challenge him.

"Then, I guess there is no other choice but to agree." Eric's man sighed and stepped back.

Only time would prove their loyalty.

EPILOGUE
A YEAR LATER

I walked throughout the pack homes, watching both women and men bustle around with smiles. The last year had been tumultuous, but things were finally settling down. Aidan and I led our pack together, and we met up monthly, rotating among the five packs that had formerly been The Hallowed Guild.

The first six months had been rough. We'd had to reemphasize our stance with the packs over and over while searching for packs that wouldn't embrace the change. The very first pack Honor and Ada hit up was their former one in Ojai, saving Honor's mother and their friends and family from the abuse. A few packs had refused to join but not nearly as many as we'd feared.

At home, a few members had left, but they'd returned months later, willing to accept the new lifestyle. It took them going out into the real world to see that what we had implemented was present everywhere.

Endora and Caleb visited the covens across the country, checking in with all of the priestesses to make sure their covens didn't feel threatened and all their needs were being met. When they returned home, they stayed with Beatrice and her coven, which had moved back to Mount Juliet.

Finn and his mother had reconnected, and I even felt like she was my family. I'd finally learned all about my biological mother and father and felt closer to them in ways I'd never thought possible. Hell, even my adopted parents treated Finn and Wanda like family. The Rogers and Murphys lived in peace. Jacob had found his fated mate and was truly happy. He apologized for trying to push our relationship for so long, and he finally understood the turmoil I felt and no longer begrudged me for my disinterest. For the first time ever, I felt complete and at ease.

"Hey, just 'cause you're the ultimate alpha doesn't mean you get to skip out on duties!" Beth hollered at me from across the road. She was with her fated mate, who happened to be part of Aidan's and my pack. I had a feeling Endora had had a hand in that.

A support beam from a porch had fallen on Beth's house last night, and Beth, her mate, and Aidan were trying to fix it.

"Fine." I called my magic, lifted the huge tree off the ground, and placed it under the roof, which was beginning to sag. "Fixed."

Beth crossed her arms. "Show off."

"Hey, you don't need to strain yourself." Aidan jogged over and kissed me. "We don't need to risk her." He placed a hand on my belly, and our baby girl kicked it.

"That won't hurt her." I gazed into his eyes and felt breathless. Every day, our bond grew stronger, which I hadn't known was possible.

"Maybe, but I have to take care of both women in my

life." His eyes were filled with so much love, and that's how I knew everything would work out. With him by my side, we could get through anything.

The End

ABOUT THE AUTHOR

Jen L. Grey is a *USA Today* Bestselling Author who writes Paranormal Romance, Urban Fantasy, and Fantasy genres.

Jen lives in Tennessee with her husband, two daughters, and two miniature Australian Shepherd. Before she began writing, she was an avid reader and enjoyed being involved in the indie community. Her love for books eventually led her to writing. For more information, please visit her website and sign up for her newsletter.

Check out my future projects and book signing events at my website.
www.jenlgrey.com

ALSO BY JEN L. GREY

The Wolf Born Trilogy

Hidden Mate

Blood Secrets

Awakened Magic

The Marked Wolf Trilogy

Moon Kissed

Chosen Wolf

Broken Curse

Wolf Moon Academy Trilogy

Shadow Mate

Blood Legacy

Rising Fate

The Royal Heir Trilogy

Wolves' Queen

Wolf Unleashed

Wolf's Claim

Bloodshed Academy Trilogy

Year One

Year Two

Year Three

The Half-Breed Prison Duology (Same World As Bloodshed Academy)

Hunted

Cursed

The Artifact Reaper Series

Reaper: The Beginning

Reaper of Earth

Reaper of Wings

Reaper of Flames

Reaper of Water

Stones of Amaria (Shared World)

Kingdom of Storms

Kingdom of Shadows

Kingdom of Ruins

Kingdom of Fire

The Pearson Prophecy

Dawning Ascent

Enlightened Ascent

Reigning Ascent

Stand Alones

Death's Angel

Rising Alpha